CHESAPEAKE & OHIO
Maintenance-of-Way Motor Cars
By Charles "Bill" Ford

© 2015

The Chesapeake & Ohio Historical Society, Inc.

Introduction to the Chesapeake & Ohio History Series Books Concept

This is the eleventh in a series of softbound books we plan to publish on a quarterly basis. Each will have a particular C&O topic that, for some reason, has not been published in such detail in our magazine. The subject matter will have a wide range: steam and diesel locomotives; passenger and freight cars; operations of all types; structures and facilities of all kinds; histories of particular areas of the line such as a city, yard, subdivision, and so forth. Readers are encouraged to make recommendations. Although we plan to issue these on a regular basis we are considering them books and not periodicals.

To subscribe to this series go to the chessieshop.com website cited below.

The Society may be contacted by writing:

The Chesapeake & Ohio Historical Society, Inc.
312 East Ridgeway Street
Clifton Forge, VA 24422

or by calling 1-540-862-2210 (Monday-Friday 9 a.m. - 5 p.m.), or by e-mail: cohs@cohs.org
The Society maintains a history information internet site at
www.cohs.org, and a full service sales site at www.chessieshop.com.

For information on The C&O Railway Heritage Center visit www.candoheritage.org

Digital Layout and Design: Michael A. Dixon
Copy Editor: Robert Jackson

International Standard Book Number: 0-939-487-00-4
Library of Congress Control Number: 2015953191

ON THE COVER: *C&O motor car No. M-20 is freshly painted and seen here at Indian Rock, Va. as C&O GP7 No. 5859 take the local freight west on May 5, 1970. (Dorr Tucker photo, C&OHS Collection, COHS 42609)*

Table of Contents

C&O HM7 hump car at Clifton Forge, Va. Motor cars were used to deliver car riders back to the top of the hump yard. (C&OHS Collection, CSPR 10684.b52)

Introduction

From an early age and through my adult life I have had an interest in railroads. While in college I discovered the C&O Historical Society but was not able to pursue my interests in the C&O until later in my life. In the 1980's having completed my college studies, I was fortunate to make many trips into C&O Railway territory with my camera to study and make observations on how the railroad operated.

My first up close encounter with a motor car came when I joined the volunteer fire department in my hometown in 1975 during my senior year of high school. My first Assistant Fire Chief Jim Naper worked for Chessie System Railroads. He was a signal maintainer who had on display in his backyard a Fairmont S2 Section Car that he had used while working for the B&O, having acquired it from the railroad when it was retired from service. Little did I know at that time, that this brief introduction to these machines would fuel a personal interest in these unique pieces of railroad equipment.

In 1983, I attended my first COHS Convention in Charleston, W. Va. where I met Thomas Dixon and Tod Hanger among others who shared my passions for the C&O. The convention was chaired by Bill Sparkmon, who became a lifelong friend and who I affectionately refer to as my other brother. After the convention I caught the C&O fever. During the 80's I served on the Board of Directors for the organization and made many trips to Clifton Forge in the early days helping the organization visualize its dream of finding a permanent home for its archival collection. The COHS is fortunate to have a large number of photos, drawings and C&O/Chessie System Company records that were given to us by Hays Watkins, who was president of Chessie System Railroads.

Like many railfans we each develop particular interests about the railroads that we are interested in and one of mine was motor cars. It was during this time I became the owner of several motor cars of C&O and N&W heritage. During my C&O trips I noticed railroad motor cars or "speeders", as they were often referred to, along the railroad property. I would see them sitting in the weeds, or around various structures, but you could sense that while some were still in use and had been around for a number of years, their time was running out. The presence of high-rail equipped trucks on the railroad was signaling the end of the road for these mighty machines.

During my many trips to Clifton Forge to the Society Headquarters I met Mr. Stewart Bostic. He was a true southern gentleman who had spent his entire life as an employee of the C&O/Chessie System Railroads in the signal department, last serving as the Supervisor of Signals in Clifton Forge. Stewart knew of my interest in the motor cars and had spent many hours riding the mountain railway in all types of adverse conditions.

Stewart in his southern voice once told me "Bill if I could get you up on that mountain in a motor car in the middle of the winter I could take that enthusiasm out of you." Stewart gave me his C&O water can from his motor car days and a brand new Fairmont Motor Car Instruction Manual in its original wrapper, that I still keep and cherish to this day even though he has passed.

My goal in this publication is to introduce the reader who is interested in the C&O Railway to understand a general history of the motor car and its importance to the growth and development of the C&O Railway. We will also explore the different types of motor cars that the C&O Railway purchased from the time period stretching from the 1920's up until the last cars were purchased in the 1980's. The Fairmont Railway Motors Company was the largest supplier of motor cars to the C&O, so a special emphasis on the company and its equipment will be covered.

As a model railroader, I am hopeful that the book will also serve as a source of ideas for adding to your layout some of these iconic machines and the related details in your efforts to recreate the C&O in miniature. After all modeling is another form of recreating history.

This book was produced with help from other individuals. First, I would like to thank Bill Sparkmon my longtime friend for his proofing of the material, Wayne Brummond of Harsco Track Technologies for being a great support in answering my questions and providing me a great deal of information, Lenny Tvedten the Director of the Martin County Historical Society where the Fairmont Collection is housed and Mary Mattox from Harsco Track Technologies for granting me permission from the Company for use of the materials in the collection. Also, thank you Harsco Track Technologies for being a corporation who thinks the past, from where you have come, is as important as where you are going into the future.

I would also like to thank Greg Michelin from NARCOA for helping me get a copy of the book by the late Leon Sapp, whom I admire, but unfortunately never had the opportunity to meet. His work on this subject was invaluable and I could not have written this without it. Thomas Dixon and Michael Dixon from the Chesapeake and Ohio Historical Society for their support of the project. I would also like to thank the NARCOA (North America Railcar Operators Association) and several of its members who provided photos and information for the book.

Lastly my wife of 35 years Jill Ford who has allowed me to pursue my railroad interests in life with her love and support and my father, John Ford, who has passed and who always supported my interests in history and railroading.

I hope you will enjoy my efforts as I tell the story about C&O "Speeders." This book is dedicated to my friend Stewart Bostic.

CHAPTER ONE

Emergence of the Railroad Maintenance-of-Way Industry

C&O track gang taking a lunch break aboard a motor car and trailer in the Clifton Forge, Va. yard complex in the Spring of 1959. (C&OHS Collection, CSPR 10684.b57)

From the first spike driven in 1828, the development of America's Railroads throughout the 1800's to the 1920's was nothing short of an explosion of expansion. While the country was in the midst of a Civil War, President Abraham Lincoln, in an attempt to keep the Pacific Coast loyal to the Union, signed into law the Pacific Railroad Act on July 1, 1862, calling for the construction of the transcontinental railroad.

The costs to complete the task were so enormous that private concerns were unable to raise the required capital for the project. In March of 1864, President Lincoln endorsed additional legislation that pledged Federal assistance to the project and with the backing of the Federal Government construction finally began. By 1869 the transcontinental railroad was completed and the golden spike was driven, and this became the catalyst for railroad projects all over the country.

Railroad mileage data for the United States from 1860-1920 illustrates the rapid and continued growth of the nation's railroads. In 1860, there were approximately 30,636 track miles and by 1870 the number of miles increased to 52,885 representing an increase in 73 percent more trackage. In 1880, the number of track miles increased to 93,671, a 77 percent increase over the previous decade.

By 1890, the number of trackage miles increased to 163,581 an increase of 75 percent in track miles nationwide. In 1900 the number of miles increased to 193,321 miles an 18 percent increase over the previous period. In 1910 there were 240,414 miles a 24 percent increase over the previous period and by 1920 there was 248,700 miles of trackage. The total percentage of trackage miles over the 60 year period increased by 712 percent.

Initially the growth and development of the C&O Railway, from its inception in 1869 to the first decade of its existence was slow. However from the period of 1888-89 the

C&O Mainline Trackage Miles	
Year	First Track Miles
1879	270
1890	931
1898	1,275
1909	1,686
1919	2,205
1929	2,259
1930	2,668 *Hocking Valley Acquired
1939	1,946
1946	2,737
1949	4,303 *Pere Marquette Acquired
1963	4,217
*Track miles does not include secondary track, sidings and yard trackage.	

railroad grew adding track miles to its inventory. The table above gives the number of track miles for the various time periods throughout the C&O Railway's existence.

For the period of 1879 to 1930 the number of trackage miles on the C&O Railway increased by 888 percent. An analysis of the same time period shows the growth in trackage was similar to increases in percentage of the national railroad trackage mileage.

In 1926 the 2nd edition of the Railway Engineering and Maintenance Cyclopedia was printed by Simmons-Boardman Publishing, which was the bible for the railroad industry. At this time the scope and size of the newly emerging Maintenance-of- Way segment of America's railroad transportation industry could be clearly seen. As of Dec. 31, 1924 the publication reported that there was 258,444 miles of trackage within the United States.

Railroad employment for the same time was at 1,750,000 employees and more than 400,000 employees of this total were working within the maintenance-of-way portion of America's railroads. The publication reported that of these 400,000 employees 250,000 were engaged directly in the maintenance of track and roadway. The expenditures for maintenance-of-way and structures on Class I railroads was estimated to be $800,000,000 dollars. This accounted for 18 percent of the total operating expenses of America's railroads.

By the time the 6th edition of the same publication was printed in 1945, using data from Dec. 31, 1943, the number of employees within the industry was listed as 1,414,200 with 295,500 employees engaged in the maintenance-of-way segment of the industry. The amount of dollars spent for maintenance-of-way and structures in 1943 was reported to be $1,108,281,000. The employment numbers of the railroads at this point were obviously affected by America being involved in World War II and many men were called up for the war forces.

There were many factors in America's railroads that made the maintenance-of-way portion of the railroad transportation industry such an important element. First, the current method of laying rail using wooden ties with fasteners on a prepared roadbed utilizes some of the same basic principles of design involved in laying railroad track that occurred with the earliest track laid in the late 1820's. When the practice of installing rail on stone pedestals imbedded in ballast without ties proved unsuccessful wooden cross ties were then placed between pedestals at various distances. When this proved not acceptable the present practice laying rail on wooden cross ties with fasteners on regular intervals became the standard for supporting the modern day railroad track and holding it to gauge.

Second, the need for a large maintenance-of-way presence within the industry was created because many of America's railroads were initially laid in great haste. Track work was poorly laid in accordance with no standards, poor drainage, light rail, poor quality rail and less than quality construction techniques. This resulted in track work that was severely impacted by the effects of mother nature and other forces. These issues required a constant presence of track work labor to maintain the poorly installed track work and roadbeds.

The ever increasing size of railroad equipment, larger and heavier locomotives driven by the desire to have greater efficiency in pulling longer, heavier trains and the increased frequency of trains over the years had a great impact on the need for additional manpower and maintenance of the railroad infrastructure. The forces delivered by reciprocating steam locomotives tended to drive the rail down and outward which had the effect of tearing apart what many men, by the sweat of their brow worked so hard to put together. When

Track gang on C&O's Pere Marquette District in Michigan raising track in 1947.
(C&O Ry. photo, C&OHS Collection, CSPR 1731)

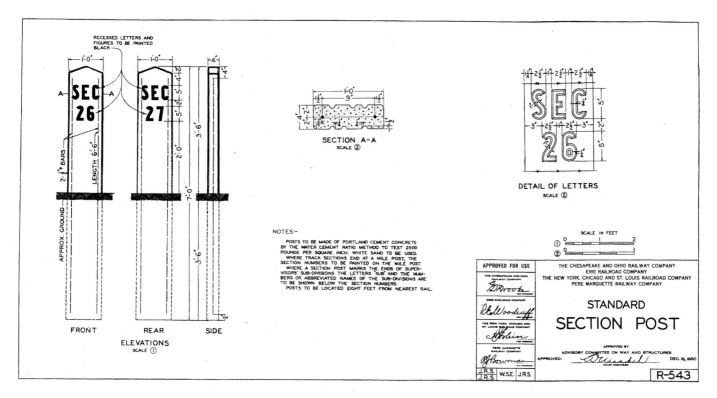

This is a joint C&O, Erie, NKP, and PM standard for concrete posts designating MofW sections.
(Sheet extracted from C&O Maintenance-of-Way Standard Drawings Vol. 1, C&O catalog number DS-7-034)

the nation entered into World War I the unprecedented traffic levels also placed a great strain on the on the railroad system.

Coupled with all of these issues the vast railroad infrastructure created by the nation's railroads was in a state of constant flux. In the early years of the C&O Railway under the direction of Collins P. Huntington from 1873 to 1988, funds for upgrading the railroad were in short supply. The railroad track work infrastructure suffered from many of the same issues that other rail lines faced.

When control of the C&O was lost to the Morgan and Vanderbilt interests in 1888-1889, under the leadership of President Melville E. Ingalls and Chief Engineer Harry Frazier an emphasis was placed upon upgrading and rebuilding the line to the highest standards. During the 1890's President Ingalls had the C&O completely rebuilt laying heavier rail replacing lightweight steel that was installed in the 1870's, ballasting roadbeds and replacing many of the wooden trestles with steel structures or eliminating bridges by constructing earthen fills. After 1900 much of the mainline routes on the C&O were laid with a second track increasing the number of track miles for the railroad in terms of maintenance.

This, coupled with Frazier's top notch engineering skills, resulted in the C&O Railway having a well constructed infrastructure that did not suffer from some of the maintenance related issues that confronted other railroads. Nevertheless, the C&O had created a first class railroad built to high standards, and it now required a large contingent of workers to maintain it in tiptop condition.

The Railroad Section Concept

To effectively maintain the track work infrastructure railroads in the United States utilized a maintenance concept which divided the railroad into maintenance sections. By the time of World War I it was estimated that there were 34,400 section gangs working on American railroads.

An article which appeared in the November, 1930 issue of the C&O Lines Magazine provides insight on how the railroads utilized this approach to build the necessary organization to address track maintenance. This system appears to have been utilized from the earliest time of the railroad industry. The section gang, as it was referred to, was the primary work unit in the railroad maintenance organization.

In this concept the railroad right-of-way was divided into numbered sections. These sections were numbered, but how the numbers were assigned to identify the various sections seems to be lost in time. The length of a section was dependent upon several factors, the volume of traffic on the line, the type of equipment that was operated over the line, whether the track was single or double track territory, and other factors affecting the difficulty required in maintaining the track in a particular section such as geography. For example, on the Northern Subdivision of the C&O which extended from the mainline connection at NJ Cabin at milepost 544 to Parsons Yard in Columbus, OH, the length of a section was established at four miles. Single track territories were typically six to ten miles in length.

Each section was assigned a Foreman who reported to the Track Supervisor. A typical section gang consisted of

C&O section gang repairing switch near Lee Hall, Va. in 1943. (C&O Ry. photo, C&OHS Collection, CSPR 41)

a workforce from three to fifteen laborers. The number of workers assigned to a section was dictated by many of the same factors that established the length of the section.

The Section Foreman and his work force had numerous responsibilities to maintain their assigned section. Their primary duties included performing all activities necessary to maintain the track work in good condition. This included keeping drainage ditches and culverts open to ensure that the right-of-way was adequately drained; removing obstructions such as landslides and falling debris from the track and ensuring track stayed in gauge and alignment to established standards. Track gauging and lining was probably the most difficult task due to weather conditions. Temperatures often caused kinks in the rail when it was extremely hot, and during extremely cold weather track pulled apart creating broken rails. Freeze and thaw cycles during and after the winter created the need for track to be surfaced and smoothed. Rail

would wear, especially in the curves, and track would move due to the forces imposed upon it by the heavy locomotives and normal forces exposed to it by the train traffic that rode the rails.

Early on the Foreman were also often times responsible for track inspection but in the later years Track Supervisors assumed these duties relieving the Foreman of this duty. The C&O also used Track Walkers, as they were often referred to, who conducted track inspections as well.

Especially in the early years prior to the 1930's and 40's section gang work involved brute physical labor. The gangs used manual tools such as lining bars, ballast forks, picks, shovels, sledge hammers, track wrenches and track tongs to carry the rail to its intended resting spot. This work was carried out in all types of environmental conditions such as extreme heat and cold. During the months when the weather was favorable the track gangs worked long, hard hours from daylight to dusk performing necessary repairs and replacing rail and ties.

The Section House

Key to the railroad section crew was the section house or tool house as it was often referred to. This was the assembly point for the section gang to report for work and these structures were located strategically along the right-of-way where the supplies and tools necessary to perform the work were located. The section houses were supplied by trains or trucks with the materials such as spikes, rail and other required items needed by the workers to maintain the track section.

The typical C&O Tool House was 12 ft. X 20 ft. in size and was located along the right-of-way at the predetermined section location. C&O Railway MW drawing 4619-C dated Dec. 21, 1937, shows the typical construction details of a

The standard C&O section house appeared at hundreds of locations across the system. This one is located at Chilesburg, Ky. on the C&O's Lexington Subdivision in 1957. (C&O Ry. photo, C&OHS Collection, COHS 2561)

section tool house for the railroad. The drawings contain a list of necessary materials that a vendor would supply which would be shipped to the planned location for the section house and the Carpenter Forces in the Maintenance-of-Way Division would erect the building at the proposed site.

An additional drawing MW 2823-B, dated Jan. 9, 1939, shows a variant of the same building which was intended for use by lineman and signal maintainers. There are differences in the two buildings and their intended uses. The interior of the two buildings differed as maintainers and lineman had an office area within the structure where this space in the typical section house provided room for a trailer or push car stored behind the motor car or hand car stored in the building. The interior arrangement for tools and supplies also differs between the two buildings.

Ideally, a section house was located in the middle of the defined work section but factors such as topography of the site to locate the building often affected the final positioning of the building within the section. Other considerations such as co-locating it with stations/cabins or other structures, the location of the Section Foreman's dwelling unit, access to a water supply source, proximity to a town and workforce and whether or not the section was supplied with a motor car were also variables in locating the building site.

C&O Railway drawing MW 1534-E dated, Aug. 17, 1928 shows the details of the layout of a section tool house and the locations of the supplies and materials. It illustrates details such as the location of underground storage tanks for oils and gasoline and a rail storage rack. It also shows a location for the storage of scrap materials on the site.

At each section house a set-off was provided to allow the railroad handcar or motor car to be put on or pulled off the track. These set-offs were fabricated using ties or timbers or other means to fill in the area between the rails at the section house so that the work crews could maneuver the motor car or hand car onto the track to and from the section house.

It is important to note that additional set-off locations were often provided at intervals along the railroad right-of-way to allow the section crews to clear up off the railroad to permit trains to pass. Typically section houses were located perpendicular to the trackage being served but there are examples on the C&O where the section house was located between multiple tracks and the section house was located parallel to the right-of-way. In this arrangement access was provided from either direction to the applicable adjacent tracks. An example of this type of arrangement was at Fort Spring, W. Va..

Section gangs were not the only crews on the railroad to have the need to store their equipment and hand or motor cars. Signal or lineman forces and other work forces on the railroad were often provided with buildings resembling section houses in which to store their handcars or motor cars. As a result, at many locations there were multiple section house type buildings to serve these various needs.

C&O GP7 No. 5815 slides by motor car set-off near Gulf Switch, W. Va. in December 1957.
(Gene Huddleston photo, C&OHS Collection, COHS 2926)

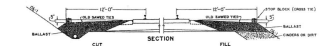

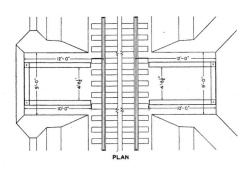

This is an extract from joint C&O, Erie, NKP, PM standard number R-527 showing how a motor car set-off is to be installed. Dated 1931. (From C&O Maintenance-of-Way and Roadway Structures - Drawings & Data Handbook, catalog number DS-01-206)

In a 1930 article written by T. S. Patterson, Assistant Division Engineer, at Chillicothe, Ohio, he goes into great detail about the need for uniformity. The buildings were designed so that by simply looking into the tool house a quick assessment of the required tools could be made as well as an inventory of needed supplies. This was important to the Track Supervisor who had to inspect the facilities under his command. The article also notes that Section Foreman may be faced with the problem of employees wanting to come to the section house during non-working hours to provide unique decorative touches which were not in the interest of uniformity, efficiency, and cost effective railroading.

Transporting Track Materials and Section Forces

The need to move men and materials to the worksite daily became a necessity with the development of the steam railroads after 1830. The traditional wagon was not always a practical means especially when the wagon routes did not follow the railroad right-of-way. This lead to the development of small flanged wheeled carts that would allow the section-man the ability to load the materials and supplies on the cart and simply push the cart to the intended work location.

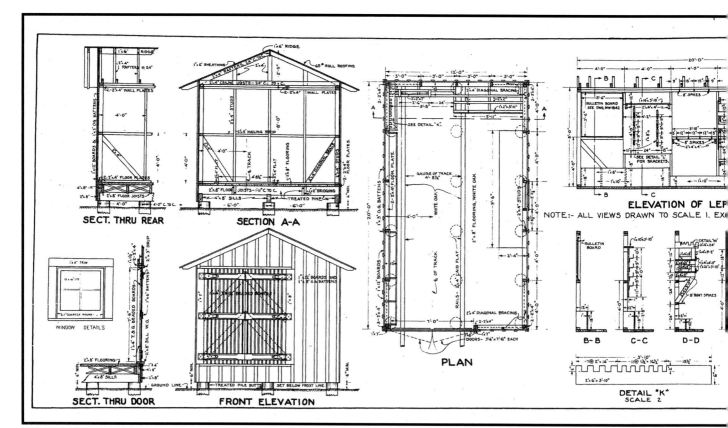

(Above) This drawing shows the standard design and arrangement for a C&O section house. This arrangement would be used by section forces. (Drawing No. MW 4619-C dated Dec. 21, 1937, revised to Oct. 21, 1948, from C&O Maintenance of Way Drawings Vol. 1, COHS catalog number DS-7-034)

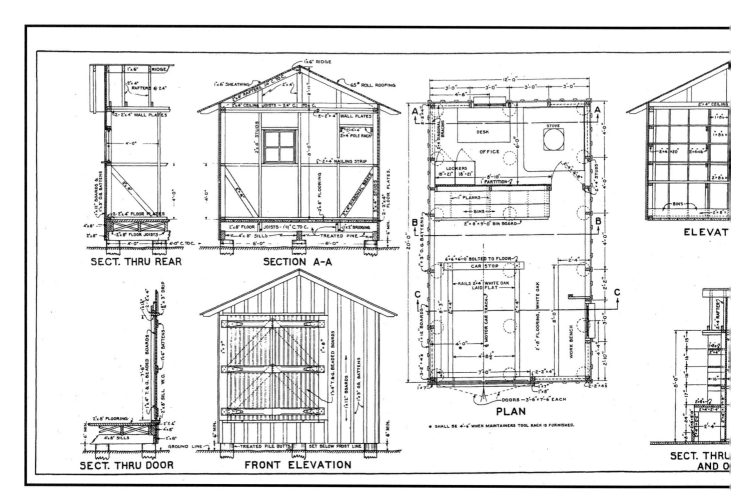

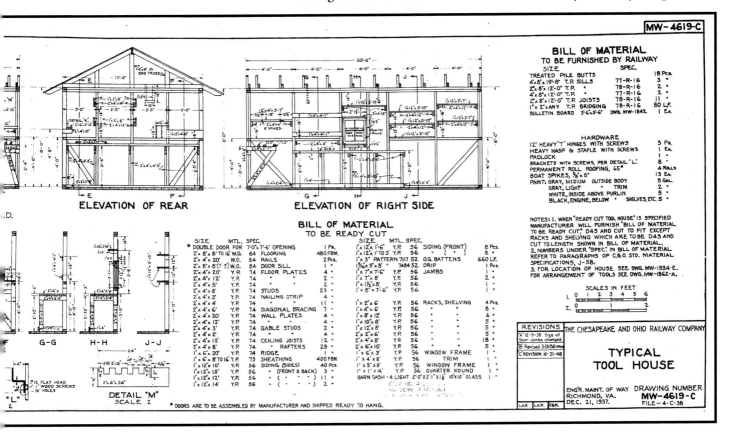

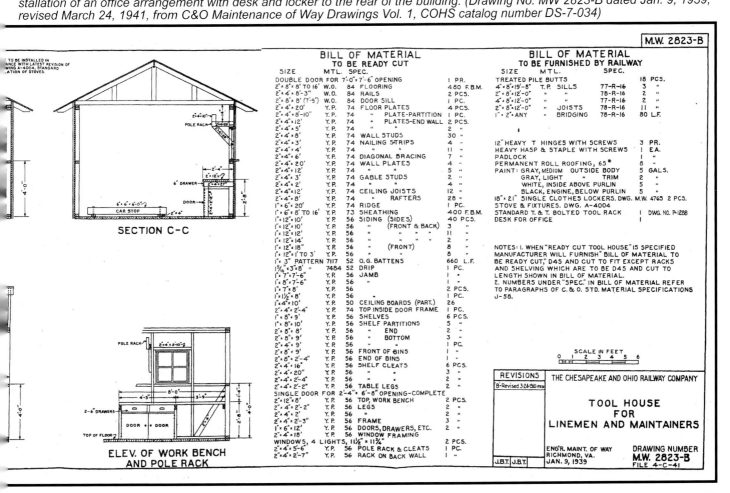

(Below) This drawing shows the arrangement of tool houses for linemen and signal maintainers which differed largely by the installation of an office arrangement with desk and locker to the rear of the building. (Drawing No. MW 2823-B dated Jan. 9, 1939, revised March 24, 1941, from C&O Maintenance of Way Drawings Vol. 1, COHS catalog number DS-7-034)

These carts are still in use on railroads today and are referred to as "push cars". In the early days it has been recorded that workers would often ride on these push cars by standing and using a long pole pushing off of the ground to propel the car down the track. This was referred to as poling them along. This method worked in the early years especially when the distance of a section was limited to a fairly small distance of three to four miles.

Other creative approaches were also recorded as being used during the mid 1800's such as sails being installed on the push cars so they could be propelled by the wind, and a car operated by the means of a pole that engaged a peg installed on the wheels of the car so that the force exerted on the pole caused the wheels to rotate. The creative minds of the American sectionman were already at work thinking there had to be a better way to get to and from the worksite location.

The next development in powered section cars came in the 1850's. It was a hand powered car similar to a bicycle except the hands were used to power the car by rotating a mechanism which transferred the energy to the wheels through a belt, chain or series of gears to propel the car. These cars were designed for both one man carts as well as larger gang type cars and lasted until the 1870's. The problem with these units was the work had to be performed by one or only a few of the members of the gang. What was needed was a mechanism which allowed more members of the gang to share in the physical work required to propel the car.

In 1861 during the beginning of the American Civil War a drawing was submitted to the U.S. Military Railroads by two men, Murphy and Allison. This was the first development of the "handcar" or "lever" car which would become the iconic symbol of the maintenance-of-way gang on Amer-

ica's railroads. These cars were used by the Union railroads during the Civil War, and at the conclusion of this war the handcar found its way into the building of the Transcontinental Railroad completed in 1869.

Each railroad section house in America was soon provided with at least one hand or lever operated car and several small push or trailer cars. There were various manufacturers of the hand car such as The Sheffield Car Co., Kalamazoo Railroad Velocipede and Car Co., Fairbanks Company and Robert, Throp and Company. The handcar would serve as the primary vehicle for section gangs for almost the next three decades.

The October, 1860 issue of the American Railway Review described a three wheel rail vehicle with a hand powered crank. Two gentlemen, Aspinwall and Perry, were awarded a patent in 1869 for converting a two wheel bicycle into a three wheel rail car. In 1878, George Sheffield designed a hand powered velocipede for himself and when he was later asked to produce more of the vehicles under contract, his company was born. Sheffield acquired the patent of Aspinwall and Perry and then obtained two other patents in his name in 1879 and 1881. He is often credited with inventing the railroad velocipede, but it is clear that the concept originated many years before. The velocipede is a three wheeled device which looks similar to a small bicycle with flanged wheels on which the rider sits above two wheels that ride on one rail and one wheel that is attached to an outrigger that rides on the other rail. The operator is seated with pegs for his feet and a lever grip arrangement that is attached to a series of gears. When the operator pulls back on the handle and then pushes it forward the reciprocating motion is transferred to the gears and to the wheels propelling the car. While the Geo. S. Sheffield Company was the first major producer of the velocipede other manufacturers also built them such as Buda Foundry and Manufacturing.

The velocipede, despite having been produced initially in the 1880's was in use on America's railroads for almost 100 years. In an article prepared for the Chesapeake and Ohio Historical Newsletter dated August, 1980, author Wesley O. Barnhart details his surprise when in May of 1974 he observed a velocipede in operation by a C&O Track Inspector on a branch of the Big Coal River Subdivision. In the article he describes talking to a relative named Bob Carver, who retired from the C&O in 1975, and had inspected track up until about a year and a half before he retired. Mr. Carver's territory covered about 95 miles of track and it took him a week to traverse the track assigned to his inspection district.

During the same period of time when the handcar and velocipedes were being used there were some attempts to build and utilize steam powered inspection and work cars. The Kalamazoo Company had built a steam powered inspection car for railroad officials in 1887 and some railroads

C&O foreman and his gang are shown en route to their job near Barboursville, W. Va. using the standard hand car which had been in use since the 1860s.
(C&O Ry. photo, C&OHS Collection, CSPR 10179.1x)

had managed to build their own equipment. In 1895, the Barnes Steam Inspection Car was a small velocipede like unit equipped with a small steam engine. The hurdles faced by the small engine were that it could not pull a trailer and it required constant vigilance to maintain the water level and steam pressure which made these devices not generally feasible. Kalamazoo did end up successfully building a steam inspection car which could carry 6-8 men and could make 30 miles per hour on level track. However the car did not really break into the maintenance-of-way market but rather it was used more by railroad officials for inspections. While a few steam inspection cars were used for laborer use they really did not catch on to any large extent.

Another option for transporting section crews to work-sites was the use of the work train. While this method was used it required a crew to staff the train, it was costly and not efficient as often times there was no place to turn the loco-motive, and the equipment would sometimes be in the way at the worksite. This clearly was not an effective or efficient way to routinely transport the men and materials to their worksites except in special situations.

In reviewing the various methods and modes for trans-porting the railroad section workers and their materials to the worksite several issues came to light that point out the relative inefficiencies that plagued the American railroads. First, a considerable amount of time was spent each day by employees traveling to and from the worksite, which was especially true when the work project for the day was located at some distant point from the section house. This time factor was then multiplied by the number of employees as-signed to the section gang which resulted in a large number of man hours that were considered non-productive. This was not necessarily a problem when labor costs were cheap but as the labor rates increased throughout the industrial devel-opment of the country and the length of the workday was reduced, railroad managers began to focus on this issue.

Also the methods used to transport the workers re-quired physical exertion. In the early years before the use of roller bearings and better mechanical design, the physical effort required to pump a handcar up a grade with a loaded trailer car of materials all had a negative effect on the physi-cal condition of the worker when they reached the worksite. This was compounded when the work was being performed in severe weather such as extreme heat or cold. Often times the employees needed a period of rest upon arrival at the worksite to recover from the exertion used to simply get them to the job in the first place.

All of these factors begged for a better way to get the work done. There is no doubt that some creative section hand had a thought when pumping the handcar on a ninety degree day in July after laying track for ten or more hours that there had to be a better way to do this without so much work!

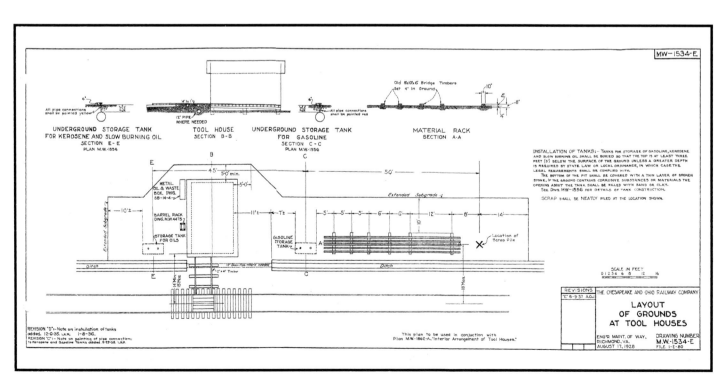

This standard drawing illustrates how supplies and materials were arranged around section tool houses. This facilitated delivery of materials by the supply train and pick up of materials to be transported to the job. (Drawing No. MW 1534-E dated Aug. 17, 1928, revised to June 9, 1937, from C&O Maintenance of Way Drawings Vol. 1, COHS catalog number DS-7-034)

This C&O three-wheel velocipede is pictured at Rum Junction, W. Va. on the Logan Subdivision. This means of conveyance was developed in the late 1800s but was still in use when this picture was taken on Sept. 2, 1972. (T. W. Dixon, Jr. photo, C&OHS Collection, COHS 40690)

C&O track walker Marshall Dixon rides his velocipede along the mainline at Catlettsburg, Ky. in December 1953. Velocipedes were often used by track walkers inspecting their particular sections of the railroad on a frequent basis. (C&O Ry. photo, C&OHS Collection, CSPR 3062)

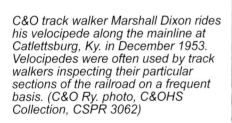

CHAPTER TWO

Development of Motorized Rail Maintenance Cars

Fairmont photo showing section gang with hand car versus a gang on an early M-2 Fairmont Gang Car. Photos carefully crafted by the Fairmont Railway Equipment Co. were a powerful sales tool. After all, which way would you have wanted to go to work? (Used with permission from Harsco Track Technologies)

The constant pressure internal combustion engine was issued a patent in 1872 to Mr. G.B Brayton of Philadelphia, Pennsylvania. He called his new device the Brayton Ready-Motor. At the time the motor was marketed in 1873 the motor was expensive and was considered to be somewhat a novelty according to author Leon Sapp in his article "Brief History of the Motorcar, Survey of the North American Manufacturers" published in the March/April 2009 issue of The Setoff.

The value of this new mechanical device was starting to be known as the device underwent further development and by 1880 an additional 18 patents had been issued. By the end of the decade an astounding 900 more patents had been issued. The internal combustion motor had firmly taken hold. In 1898 the *Gas, Gasoline and Oil Vapor Engines'* Magazine listed 62 manufacturers of such equipment but by 1906 there were 541. Some early manufacturers of these small engines were Baldwin, Buda, Stover Westinghouse and the Fairmont Machine Company, which was the predecessor to the present day Fairmont Railway Motors Company.

By the turn of the century the number of manufacturers grew rapidly and small motors were primarily being used as stationary motors to power rural America, in agricultural

and oil field use, and powering machine shops and saw mills in industrial use. Eventually they were marketed for domestic uses such as for powering wash machines and the units could be purchased through the catalog at Montgomery Wards. The gasoline motor had clearly taken hold in America.

As these little motors became readily available, industrious section workers converted their hand operated section cars by dispensing of the hand lever assembly and adding a belt or chain drive to allow the newly developed small motors perform the laborious work of powering the section handcar. No longer did the section hand have to provide the energy to get him to and from his place of designated work, within his section on the railroad.

These individual efforts ultimately lead to the development of the motorized railway motor car. There is much debate about who actually produced the first unit, but it appears that in 1892 Mr. W.G. Besler claimed to have assembled one for a superintendent on the CB&Q Railroad utilizing a Buda gas engine and a chain drive. Another individual, D.C. Stover, claimed about the same time to have built one for an official on the Illinois Central Railroad.

Brayton Pertoleum engine image from Gas & Oil Engines *by Dugald Clerk in 1886.*

Information in an article in Jan. 13, 1893 of The Railroad Gazette suggests that the Motter Manufacturing Company of Springfield, Ohio, began manufacturing a small motor car and that several had been already utilized on Southern railroads. A drawing published in the 1895 issue of Locomotive Engineering shows a motor car with a spring type buggy seat on the car equipped with a third seat in the rear for the operator. The drawing illustrates that the unit was manufactured on a handcar type frame.

In 1893, The Daimler Manufacturing Company, headed by the European inventor Gottlieb Daimler, may have been one of the first companies to produce a motorized rail motor car. Daimler, working with another German inventor, Wilhelm Maybach, in 1885 designed a gas motor specifically for the automobile which abandoned the traditional motor design that utilized a horizontal engine with an external flywheel. They took their early design and perfected the carburetor and in 1887 purchased a small plant to produce the engine. Daimler was also partnered with the piano maker Steinway to make wooden boat and rail passenger bodies, that could be installed on his newly developed engines. In 1893 Steinway convinced him to display at the 1893 World's Fair a small railcar that he had manufactured for trolley railways. The street railroads had, however, been disappointed with an earlier gas combustion product produced by the Connelly Company so his new product was not well received.

Daimler was not discouraged and in 1894 he arranged for the manufacturing of a four passenger railroad inspection car which was manufactured in Kalamazoo, Michigan. The car was basically a lightweight version of his automobile and the unit was displayed at the American Institute Fair held at Madison Square Garden in the same year. Powered by a 2hp motor with a patented closed loop water system for cooling, the car was designed to operate at speeds of 7 or 15 miles per hour, however there is no record that any of these cars were actually sold in the United States. Daimler did go on in 1896 under the newly formed Daimler Motor Company to produce some seven persons passenger vehicles, which were used by the British railways with limited success.

The Buda Foundry and Manufacturing Company which was started in 1876, but not incorporated until 1881, was

Pere Marquette section gang poses with their early motor car around 1920. The typical section gang motor car could carry six to eight men to the worksite. (C&O Ry. photo, C&OHS Collection, CSPR 1774)

Mudge Section Car Top For Old Hand Cars

Assembled Complete With Engine—Belt and Pulley
THE "WONDER-PULL" CLASS GQ-2
Wide Seat Board—6 Horse Power—Weight 300

Where good sound hand or push cars are now in service they can be quickly transformed into first class section cars with the Mudge "Wonder-Pull."

In addition to the complete frame and engine with all parts assembled a 14" diameter split steel pulley is furnished with 4" weather proof Gandy belt.

The equipment is located on car directly over center sills and with the bolts that are furnished is securely fastened to longitudinal and cross sills.  There is no chance to make improper installation. Plenty of seating room provided, no holes cut for engine parts. Engine is at the side and accessible.

The work of mounting can be done in a short time by Foreman and his men. It is not necessary to ship cars into shop for re-building and no extra parts are required therefore, there is *no additional expense* for labor or material.

This is an important feature for you to consider.

Your Men do the Work Quickly at tool house

Standard equipment is constructed without starting crank. This feature is furnished as an extra where required. For some classes of service the starting crank is very desirable. After engine has been started belt is tightened to get under way.

Equipment With Crank

Either kerosene or gasoline can be used as fuel. Kerosene equipment is fitted with double compartment tank and two tubes. Engine starts on gasoline then burns kerosene. If this feature is desired it should be specified when ordering.

You can haul heavier loads than this with the Mudge

Engine parts interchangeable with those on the G-2 Inspection Car and GS-2 and GS-4 Section Cars. Purchase Mudge equipments for your men and all Seat Tops and frame parts used by your section men will be standard. This includes coils, switches, wiring, etc. Not a different type of seating arrangement on each hand car built from available odds and ends.

Write Service Department for more information and recommendations for use.

Mudge motorizing kit for hand cars. (Used with permission from Harsco Track Technologies)

founded in Buda, Illinois. The company built small internal combustion engines for stationary use. Early on the company moved to the Chicago suburb of Harvey, Illinois and built traditional hand cars, and velocipedes as well as small motors. In a March 1942 article in Railroad Magazine author Bob White wrote, that in 1893 the Buda Foundry & Manufacturing Company was the first company to market a readymade section motor car. This car was actually a Buda Motor Velocipede where one of their small engines was mounted on one of their velocipede units with a direct drive to the motor. The unit was intended for a single rider, but the car could be modified to accommodate up to two additional workers.

Shortly after the 1893 release of the Buda motor velocipede the Kalamazoo Railway Equipment Company released its own commercial model. By 1895 Buda was producing larger section type cars as commercially manufactured units as opposed to a motorizing kit being retrofitted on a hand car. When by 1896 a joint effort by Sheffield-Fairbanks launched their first motorized cars, it was clear that the seed for manufactured motor cars had taken hold.

Regardless of who gets credit for the production of the first rail motor car, by the decade of the 1890's a change was imminent that would make the average section workers job much easier. Transportation to and from the worksite was no longer going to be the physical challenge that it had been since the dawn of railroads.

Even with these developments non-motorized handcars and velocipedes remained in use for the next two decades.

Most of these units however ended up being rebuilt into motorized units by their users and ultimately became motor cars. Non-motorized cars were still manufactured up to the period of the World War II era as many of them were exported to underdeveloped countries where gasoline was as not readily available.

During this initial period from 1895 to 1910 the focus was on the sales and manufacture of motorizing kits designed to convert the traditional handcars and velocipedes into powered self-propelled units freeing the section worker from the task of propelling his vehicle. By the turn of The Twentieth Century the number of manufacturers of the equipment was growing. During the period of 1910 through 1920 the number of companies producing motor cars and motorizing kits was the greatest of anytime during the history and development of the motor car. Author Leon Sapp in his book *The North American Railroad Section Car*, has identified over 60 manufacturers of equipment related to the motor car. During this period he estimated that two thirds of these companies built only motorizing kits for re-powering the velocipede and hand cars rather than manufacturing complete motor cars. Many of these companies came and went and were in business for only a short period. More of these companies would later leave the market as the demand for the motorizing kits waned in favor of commercially produced units.

In the 1890-1920 period in the industry the cost for a new motor car was not proportional to the worker's salary. Even in 1911 the average wage of a track laborer was

C&O trackwalker on velocipede on Big Sandy Subdivision in 1954. (C&O Ry. photo, C&OHS Collection, CSPR 10025.317)

somewhere around 25 cents per hour making his monthly wage approximately $50.00. The Section Foreman's pay was around $65.00 monthly, and a the salary of a Roadmaster, who was an official, would have been $90.00 to $100.00 monthly depending upon the railroad by which he were employed. As a result a motorizing kit was much more a reality to the average section worker than a new motor car. If the individual employee could not afford it, then a salesman could surely focus on the entire gang to see if collectively they could raise the funds needed to purchase a motorizing kit.

In 1904 the The Scientific American Reference Book reported there were approximately 239,166 section laborers in the U.S. with 33,817 Section Foremen. Using these statistics it appears that each Section Foreman averaged six laborers in the gang assigned to him. If each gang had at least one handcar, there were quite a few motorizing kits to be sold by the salesmen. There are even stories where the Section Foreman assessed section gang workers a portion of their weekly wages to pay for the motoring kit since the railroads were not providing them.

Therefore the focus for these new products during the early years of the motor car and motorizing kits was selling the product to the individual railroad section worker and not to the railroads themselves. The reason was that there were two factors in play at the time: First remember that the internal combustion engine was still relatively new and the railroads were firmly committed to the concept of steam power; and second the railroads had not yet bought into the need of providing the cars as tools for the workers.

In the early years of American labor there was a concept that an individual employee, as part of their growth and development within their individual craft, was responsible for acquiring their own tools for performing their job. As one progressed from the apprentice level to a journeyman in his trade he was expected to obtain the needed tools to perform the job and they were not generally provided by the employer. This concept most probably carried over as well to the railroad laborer in the early years and as a result there was no expectation that the railroad would provide a motor car for the employees.

As these new manufacturers started marketing the motorizing kits the companies often provided financing plans for the purchases of such equipment. If your employer allowed you to apply the kit to their company supplied handcar you could often buy a motorizing kit for $5.00 down and with monthly payments of $5.00 without interest. For example, a motorizing kit from the Elgin Wheel and Engine Company was available at the cost of $29.95 to motorize a velocipede and a Casey Jones Kit to motorize a handcar was available for $85.00 cash or $90.00, if purchased with credit with $5.00 monthly installments.

Even with the relatively low wages in these early years, it must have been a successful strategy for the equipment suppliers, because the number of companies that provided the kits swelled. They had found a willing market and soon the ads for the kits started appearing in all of the trade journals and union publications.

Companies like the Chicago Pneumatic Tool Company advertised "Don't Pump Your Life Away", the Buda Company proclaimed "Pay As You Ride" and the North Western Company advertised "Why Pump the Old Hand Car When You Can Ride In Comfort On A Motor Car" in their sales ads. Clearly American Capitalism and salesmanship had taken hold in the motor car industry!

A November 1907 article in the Railway Age magazine endorsed the motor car as being a required item which permitted better inspections resulting in greater public protection. During 1909 and 1910 major Midwest railroads such as the Chicago, Milwaukee and Saint Paul Railroad and the Chicago Great Western Railroads reported the savings resulting from the use of the motor car. In September 1911 an article in industry trade publication, the Railroad Age Gazette, read by many officials in the railroad industry, published an article "Motor Hand Cars for Section Use". By 1912 the Santa Fe Employee Magazine contained an article on powered motor cars. It indicated that during that year 500 Rockford cars had been placed into service on the Santa Fe Railroad and the same article discussed how a motor car freed the employee of the need to pump a handcar and kept them fresh for the day's work to come.

Even actions by the government helped to bring about acceptance of the machines. During 1915 the U.S. Department of Agriculture purchased four motor cars from three different manufacturers, Mudge-Adams, Buda and Fairbanks Morse ranging from $187.00 to a high of $245.00. The Department of Commerce also purchased two powered velocipedes for use in the National Coast and Geodetic Survey conducted over a five year period from 1916 to 1920.

In 1916 the Railway Signal Engineer magazine published an article, which indicated that a motor car should be the first priority for a railroad company to provide to its signal forces. It was becoming obvious that the opinion of the railroad industry relative to the necessity of the motor car was beginning to change.

Congress indirectly supported the railroad motor car by passing the Adamson Act of 1916, which established an eight-hour workday for railroad employees. Another government action establishing the U.S. Railroad Administration, when the country entered World War I, also indirectly supported the motor car. Under government control the railroads were freely permitted to purchase motor cars and in 1918, when the Railroad Administration dictated a substantial increase in the rate of pay for maintenance-of-way workers, this also had an indirect effect. The increase resulted in a 25% wage increase for Roadmasters, a flat $25.00 increase for Section Foremen and a 12 cent-per-hour increase for the section laborer. These rates represented a substantial increase when you consider the national average wage for the laborer was 25 cents- per-hour in 1911, only seven years earlier.

Fairmont Railway Equipment photo showing one man lifting a motor car off of the track.
(Used with permission from Harsco Track Technologies)

World War I also brought about a labor shortage in the section gang forces forcing railroads to look at ways to deal with the reduced size of the section gangs. This required the railroads to look at ways to maintain the amount of work performed with fewer people.

The Transportation Act of 1920, which created the Railroad Labor Board, changed the dynamics of how the railroads would handle future negotiated labor contracts. Maintenance-of-way contracts did not typically dictate crew sizes as were common in the operating units of the railroad. The use of motor cars was seen as one way to maintain the railroad track infrastructure with smaller gangs by improving the efficiency of the smaller units.

During this time period between 1910 and 1920 the railroads themselves began to recognize and accept the motor car. The words efficiency and cost savings seemed to be reoccurring themes in the various trade and railroad publications of the time.

This change in attitude by railroad management was also being sensed by the industry which produced the motorizing kits and the new motor car products. The industry saw that what was typically a sale of one car or motorizing kit at a time to the individual worker could have the potential to become a much larger proposition. To achieve this potential the motor car industry recognized that it had to address several issues if it were to successfully bring railroad officials and the railroad industry in general fully on board. The issues that needed to be addressed were as follows.

First railroad officials had to be convinced that the motor car meant greater efficiency in the use and effectiveness of the workforce. In the era of World War I, a Northwestern Motor Company ad stated "Times have changed lately. A crew of men can not be picked up whenever needed as heretofore. With almost a million men called by the Government, and the industries and agricultural interests operating to full capacity, it is but natural that men do not feel like pumping a hand car when they can get easier work at the same wages....". Clearly the company was causing railroad officials, already feeling the strain of war in securing adequate labor forces, to think that this would help to keep their current labor forces or give them the ability to attract laborers in a tight competitive labor market. The same ad stated "It lightens the labor, and makes play of the hardest part of the day's work. It stands for much greater efficiency with the same crew". Even after the conclusion of the war and increased labor pool availability, the concept of doing more with less and the seeds of how the motor car could promote greater workforce efficiency had been planted. In later years this efficiency translated into the increased size of section

A lever hand car and hand crank car manufactured by the Jackson and Sharp Company.
(Used with permission from Delaware Public Archives)

territories for the Roadmaster, who now had the ability to supervise and inspect a larger territory. The motor car also allowed Track Inspectors to cover larger sections.

Next railroad officials had to be sold on the use of gasoline as a fuel. The railroad industry had long used kerosene in the marker lights on cabooses, in lanterns and for switch stand markers. Kerosene existed in the supply chain already within the railroad industry and each location generally had a ready quantity of the product available. To make gasoline readily available at the various railroad sites meant that the railroad managers would have to develop another supply chain. Gasoline was also more costly than kerosene, selling at 10 cents a gallon versus kerosene at 7 cents per gallon.

Safety was another consideration. Kerosene with a flashpoint at around 104 degrees was generally safer to handle and use than gasoline with its flashpoint of only -45 degrees. While some manufacturers made small motors designed to run on the much more available kerosene, they did not really take hold. This occurred despite two companies, Fairbanks-Morse and Mudge, displaying kerosene cars in their equipment displays in 1918 at the Railway Appliances Exhibition. The problem with kerosene engines was that to burn efficiently, the engine had to be hot and for the short distances that the motor cars often traveled the engine did not become sufficiently heated, resulting in poor motor performance. To overcome this some manufacturers even supplied motor cars with two fuel tanks, one with gasoline and the other kerosene. The operator was instructed to operate the car on gasoline until the engine was heated up before switching to the less volatile kerosene.

The next area of consideration for convincing the railroad officials of the value of the motor car was related to the reliability and design of the cars themselves. Historically, section workers were limited to using hand tools, so, the manufacturers had to convince the railroad officials that the cars they designed could be operated by existing section forces without creating a new class of employee. In short, the technology had to be simple. They also had to be designed for cheap and easy operation and be easily repaired without having to be sent back to specially equipped shops which would have to be created to repair and maintain the machines. Kalamazoo Railway Equipment Company ads stated that: "they are designed to give maximum service with a minimum of repairs" when referring to their line of motor cars. Buda ads stated "Is Simple Enough for a Boy to Operate." Fairmont referred to their line of motor cars in a 1913 ad as "The Mighty Fairmont." Cleary the manufacturers were trying to convince the railroad officials that their simple reliable products could be used by the common laborer and that they were rugged little machines.

After the railroads however committed to providing the units for their maintenance-of-way operations, most railroads found that they had to provide system-wide repair shops. On the Chesapeake and Ohio for example, the main shop was located at the C&O Reclamation Plant in Barboursville, West Virginia. At many major terminals such as Hinton, West Virginia and Clifton Forge, Virginia, motor car shops were also provided. Despite the fact that the machines were rugged units they were often used under harsh conditions. Accidents that required major rebuilding and repairs also occurred with the units. Motor cars that needed more than the typical light repair and general servicing in the field were sent back to these specialty shops for restoration and repair.

Lastly, ease of use was an extremely important factor in pushing for the acceptance of the motor car. Manufacturers, through literature and advertising photos, often showed photos of one man easily lifting and setting a car on or off the track. This was accomplished by the use of the extension handles, which allowed one man to maneuver a 500 pound motor car with little effort. This was particularly important where only one man was operating a car and the car had to be set off the track at the work site or to be set off to allow a train to safely pass.

Repairing motor cars in the motor car shop at C&O Reclamation Plant in Barboursville, W. Va. in 1948. (C&O Ry. photo, C&OHS Collection, CSPR 1843)

CHAPTER THREE

Motor Car Design Evolves

Fairmont Model A2 gang car pulling two loaded TT20 trailer cars loaded with workers on Aug. 4, 1927. (Used with permission from Harsco Track Technologies)

As introduced in Chapter Two, the railroad motor car evolved from the application of small motors, which had been designed for the agricultural and industrial markets, to hand powered section cars to eliminate the task of the physical labor of pumping a velocipede or handcar to the worksite by the railroad laborer. This was initiated by the workers themselves to improve their own work situation.

From 1900 until the mid-1920's the motor car was refined and the industry changed its focus from providing motorizing kits to repower the velocipede and hand car to producing purpose-built machines. As these changes took place the units themselves began evolving to suit the various purposes for which they were built.

The second edition of the Railway Engineering and Maintenance Encyclopedia, published in 1926 by the Simmons-Boardman Publishing Company, divided motor cars into three classes: inspection cars; section cars; and extra gang cars. The inspection cars were the lightest cars intended for a single operator, but they could be modified to carry up

to three persons. The section car was the intermediate car between the inspection and extra gang car which was the heaviest unit. In contrast, the 6th edition published in 1945, divided motor cars into six classifications. The classifications now included the following: light inspection cars; inspection cars; light section cars; standard section cars, heavy-duty section cars and extra gang cars. This reclassification of motor cars into further categories was reflective of the further design changes to the cars and the fact that the cars were being built more for a specific use in the field.

The 1926 reference book for railroad officials listed seven manufacturers of railroad motor cars: Adams, Buda, Fairmont, Kalamazoo, Mudge, Northwestern and Sheffield.

By 1945, only four manufacturers were listed in the publication, Buda, Fairbanks-Morse, Fairmont and the Kalamazoo Railway Supply Company. The Sheffield Company and its product line had been acquired by the Fairbanks-Morse Company and Fairmont had acquired the Mudge Company in 1928. The Adams Motor and Manufacturing Company

Model No. 59 inspection car that is a side-load car intended for one or two men. Notice the engine is not centered between the rails. Many early motor cars were side-loaded types. Photo dated Dec. 26, 1930.
(Used with permission from Harsco Track Technologies)

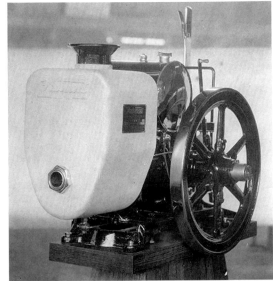

Fairmont QB two-cycle, water-cooled engine. Photo dated Dec. 29, 1924.
(Used with permission from Harsco Track Technologies)

had been acquired by the Woolery Machine Company in 1940. Northwestern suspended motor car production when World War II broke out and manufactured items only for the war effort, but in 1945 after the war they returned again to producing motor cars.

The early inspection cars were light units, which were side loaded because they were developed out of the motorization of the velocipede. The first cars of this type were generally outfitted with a four-cycle motor and were direct drive units. Since the units lacked a transmission and were not reversible they could be propelled in only a forward direction. The car would have to be lifted off of the rails and turned around in order to travel in the other direction. The cars were very light and were push started.

At the turn of the century, the early section cars were generally provided with a one or two-cylinder power plant which could be either air or water cooled. The drive mechanism powered the unit through a chain drive to the axle which was controlled with a friction disc or planetary type transmission.

Around 1908 the two-cycle engine underwent further development and refinement and this improved engine offered some distinct advantages as a power plant for the motor car. First, the two-cycle motor was reversible and could be run in either direction, which eliminated the need for the transmission with its chains and sprockets. In their place was a drive belt to transfer the power from the motor to the axle and this greatly simplified the design of the car. The two-cycle motor was also a much simpler engine mechanically with less parts internally since it did not have valves, cams, springs etc. This made it simpler to produce and maintain and achieved greater efficiency in fuel use.

Despite these improvements some manufacturers stayed with their individual preferences and each debated the advantages of their product such as water cooled versus air

cooled engines, two-cycle versus four-cycle and belt-driven versus transmission and chain drive.

Around 1910 inspection and section cars were equipped with engines ranging in the 3-5 hp. range and the transmission types were direct, belt-driven and chain-driven. Horizontal engines had taken over as the vertical engine design had proved unsuitable.

Further designs of transmissions to provide greater pulling power had been developed and the designs were moving away from the direct coupled transmission. This allowed the engines to be started without a load on them and eliminated the dangerous condition of having men run with a car in order to start them. This practice was especially dangerous when the motor car was pulling a loaded trailer. Eliminating the direct coupled transmission could be achieved by using one of several design methods. One method was a belt drive with an idler pulley that could be used so that the belt was free of the engine until the belt lever was depressed taking the slack out of the belt, causing friction on the rear axle pulley to propel the car. The slacked belt had the net effect of being a clutch mechanism. Fairmont early on adopted this method of propulsion on their inspection and section cars while Adams, a manufacturer who was in business until 1940, held on to the direct drive car propulsion system for their cars.

Another power transmission design was the use of a friction disc transmission, in which a wheel referred to as the drive wheel, was mounted on the shaft of the motor and another wheel would be brought into contact with the drive wheel at ninety-degrees. By moving the second wheel along the face of the drive wheel, the speed could be varied and the direction of travel controlled to provide both forward and reverse. A belt or chain could then be used to transfer the power from the shaft of the second wheel to the axle of the motor car. This drive method could be used on motor cars

An early belt-driven Fairmont motor car being started with the hand crank.
(Used with permission from Harsco Track Technologies)

with four-cycle engines since the engines could not be run in reverse like their two-cycle counterparts.

An advantage of the friction disc transmission was that the engine speed could remain constant since the position of the wheel as it moved across the face of the drive wheel had the effect of changing the speed. Since the motor was running at a constant speed this permitted full power at the start of motion. However one problem with this type of system was that the drive wheel had to remain clean and dry for the unit to perform as designed; a problem in the railroad environment of those days.

The Buda Company by 1906 was utilizing the friction disc type of drive mechanism on large gang sized motor cars, which utilized a twin cylinder, air-cooled motor with the friction disc and chain drive. However, they did not patent the design and the Sheffield Company then obtained a patent for a friction driven car. Sheffield then sued the Buda Company claiming their design was a patent infringement, and the Buda Company counter-sued. After an initial court ruling in favor of Sheffield, Buda was able to win an appeal in 1911 which got the Sheffield patent thrown out.

Another drive system used was one in which the drive engine was mounted on a sliding base that could be repositioned so that slack was introduced in the drive belt. This allowed the engine to remain free until the engine was started.

When the engine was relocated on the sliding base, the slack was eliminated and power was transferred from the engine to the axle pulley. Horace E. Woolery one of the founders of the Fairmont Machine Company obtained patents for this sliding base type of engine mount.

Right rear view of a BM-19 Farimont Motor car with sliding base engine and belt drive taken on Jan. 28, 1927.
(Used with permission from Harsco Track Technologies)

Demountable 20-1/4" wheel on an S2 motor car being installed on hub by a worker. Photo dated Aug. 1, 1929. (Used with permission from Harsco Track Technologies)

section and extra gang motor cars. This design was seen as more favorable as the center of gravity was centered over the track and the weight was evenly distributed on wheels and axles.

In the section car classification in the mid 1920's, the belt driven, one-cylinder, two-cycle, water-cooled driven car with a belt was the design of choice. These cars weighed somewhere between 750 to 1,000 pounds in weight and typically seated 6-8 men.

The heavier section classifications and extra gang car used transmissions of the friction type with a combination of chain and sprocket drives. These cars performed in heavy-duty usage pulling large numbers of trailer cars, with many riders, and pulling push carts with materials loaded on them.

The gang cars during the early years were equipped with 6 to 8 hp. rated engines, but by the 1930's these cars were equipped with four-cylinder engines, three and four speed transmissions and were capable of pulling as many as seven trailers. The horsepower could range from as little as 15 to as much as 72. Many of these cars received standard truck or

Many of these developments in the various propulsion means were made just prior to the period leading up to World War I. During this same period around 1914 a larger 8 hp motor was developed for the motor cars and the use of roller bearings became the standard. The water-cooled engine utilizing an aluminum hopper designed to prevent bursting in freezing weather eventually won out, but the various manufacturers would still have differing viewpoints over the merits of a water-cooled engine versus an air-cooled unit.

By the mid 1920's the standard inspection car design started to move away from the side-load style car in favor of the center-load design car. However many of the older side-load cars were still in service where the number of workers to be carried was few and the cars were typically being used for track inspection, signal maintenance and other light duty uses. The side-load style motor car, was preferred by some railroads due to its extremely light weight of which some weighed only 350 pounds. This permitted the easy removal from the track especially when the car was occupied by only one worker. The side-load style car was usually provided with a tool tray and many were still direct drive powered units. The earliest of these cars were powered by one or two-cycle engines, that were typically air-cooled engines.

One problem with the side-loaded motor car was if the load weight was not properly distributed the car could be less stable on the track and more susceptible to derailing. Eventually the side load cars were replaced with center-load designed cars, the design which ultimately prevailed for the

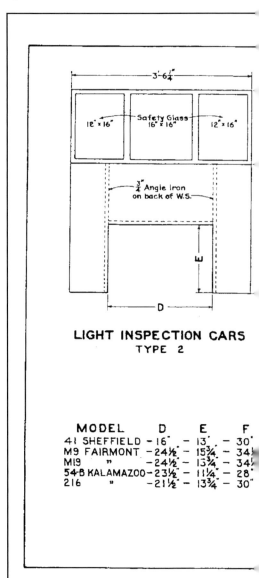

LIGHT INSPECTION CARS
TYPE 2

MODEL	D	E	F
41 SHEFFIELD	16"	13"	30"
M9 FAIRMONT	24½"	15¾"	34"
M19 "	24½"	13¾"	34"
54-B KALAMAZOO	23½"	11¼"	28"
216 "	21½"	13¾"	30"

automobile type transmissions instead of the earlier friction drive types. They had truly become workhorses with that much power.

Many manufacturers also provided power takeoffs that allowed powered hand tools to be used by the laborer at the job site. Motor car manufacturers also produced specialty equipment such as generator cars that could be towed to the site to assist with the work of the section hands.

Many advertising photos from the motor car manufacturers showed these extra gang cars pulling strings of trailers with the ads touting that they pulled a gang of 75 to 100 workers. These very powerful advertising images no doubt impressed the railroad officials in charge of purchasing equipment for maintenance-of-way forces looking to improve the efficiency and effectiveness of their workforces.

Over the years basic motor car machines were developed, refined, and evolved into new designs. In 1929 Fairmont introduced the demountable wheel for use on motor cars which offered three distinct advantages. First it allowed

for interchangeability so that the railroads would not have to stock multiple types of wheels within their inventory and supply chain. As an example, in 1936 Fairmont equipment utilized seven different types of wheels. With the exception of the 14" X 1/4" wheel used on their light inspection cars, the M9 and M59, the other six types of wheels all used the same demountable mounting hub. Second, with the demountable wheel only the tire was changed and discarded with the wheel hub remaining.

Third and most importantly, the demountable wheel made changing a wheel in the field simpler by the local forces. This was because the demountable hubs remained in place in proper gauge so that neither the gauge of wheels nor the insulating bushing on the axles were disturbed. Insulating bushings were installed on motor cars to make them electrically isolated so that they would not trip signal detection circuits or crossing signals. Changing of a wheel could be performed in the field in approximately 15 minutes with minimal tools eliminating the need for a motor car to be returned to a motor car shop for repair.

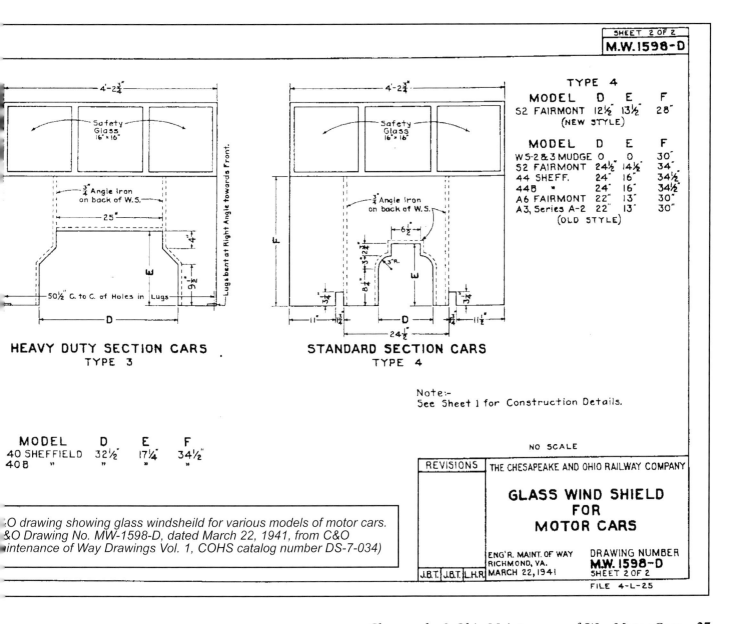

(C&O drawing showing glass windsheild for various models of motor cars. C&O Drawing No. MW-1598-D, dated March 22, 1941, from C&O Maintenance of Way Drawings Vol. 1, COHS catalog number DS-7-034)

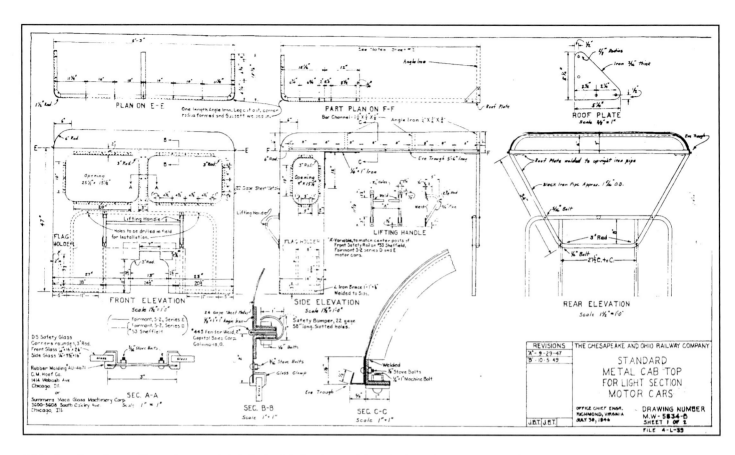

This drawing shows dimensions and details for fabrication and installation of steel cabs on C&O motor cars.
(C&O Drawing No. MW-5834-B sheets 1 and 2, dated July 30, 1946, revised to Oct. 5, 1949, from C&O Maintenance of Way Drawings Vol. 1, COHS catalog number DS-7-034)

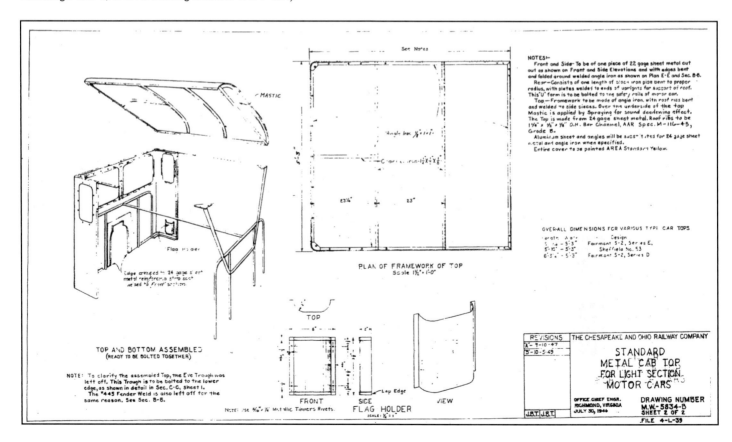

An M9-G crated for shipment to the C&O with Fairmont steel V-Nose style cab and curtains on Apr. 2, 1948. (Used with permission from Harsco Track Technologies)

The use of riveted and other types of wheels prior to the advent of the demountable wheel often meant that the car had to be taken out of service and returned to a motor car repair facility to simply replace a wheel. The out-of-service car also caused work production issues and logistics issues for the railroad.

The electrical systems in the early motor cars were very basic systems. They consisted of a battery ignition using dry cells with a spark coil box or a magneto which were similar to those used on early automobiles. These provided the necessary electrical supply to operate the engine. By April of 1937, Fairmont was offering generators with voltage regulation and a storage battery for its motor cars which paved the way for the application of lights to permit operation at night. Prior to the application of generators on the motor cars, early headlights were separate dry-celled power units. Other improvements to motor cars during this time period consisted of the application of windshields to shield the men from the harsh winter winds. There are numerous photos of C&O cars where section forces fashioned their own such assemblies out of plywood and other materials.

No doubt the manufacturers of the motor cars saw these items being added to their cars in the field and designed a product to meet the need. The C&O MW Drawing 1598-D, produced in 1941 details the construction of a glass windshield for application to the various types of motor cars that were in the fleet at the time.

Sheet 2 of this drawing shows the dimensions for three classifications of motor cars and refers to them as Type 2, light inspection cars, Type 3 heavy duty inspection cars and Type 4 standard section cars.

<u>Light Inspection Cars Type 2</u>
Sheffield	Model 41
Fairmont	M-9
Fairmont	M-19
Kalamazoo	216
Kalamazoo	M54-B

<u>Heavy Duty Section Cars Type 3</u>
Sheffield	Model 40
Sheffield	Model 40B

<u>Standard Section Cars Type 4</u>
Fairmont	S-2
Mudge	WS-2&3
Sheffield	Model 44
Sheffield	Model 44B
Fairmont	A6
Fairmont	A3
Fairmont	A2

Later these simple windshields were enhanced to provide cab tops for the motor cars with side curtains to further protect the workers from the elements.

What is significant about this drawing is that it lists the manufacturer and model type of the cars within each class, and clearly shows in the early years that the C&O bought motor cars from several manufacturers. It also shows that the C&O was producing these after-market items in its own shops rather than ordering such products from the manufacturers. The C&O however did purchase some cars with cabs installed by Fairmont between the late 1930's to the mid 1940's.

This is not surprising given the fact that at Barboursville, West Virginia where the main motor car shops were located, there was also a tin shop, sewing shop and carpenters shop. The C&O had all of the resources in place to manufacture these items internally. Since many of these cars were in the inventory well before the accessories became available from the various manufacturers, it simply made sense to produce the items in house.

Another drawing in the COHS archive collection is MW-5834-B, sheets 1 and 2, that show the development of a standard steel cab roof top for the light section motor cars. This drawing, dated July 30, 1946, gives details for the construction of a cab roof to be applied to the Fairmont S2, Series E, S2 Series D and Sheffield Model 53 car. Photos in the COHS archives and others in the author's collection show that cab roofs were installed on other smaller inspection cars such as the Fairmont M9 and M19. What is interesting is that a Fairmont official photo in the company collection shows an S2, Series F section car in January of 1947, ready to ship to the C&O with a factory applied cab. This cab looks similar to the C&O drawings that were created in July of 1946. It makes you wonder if this car was the prototype that was ordered after the design of the cab was prepared by the C&O.

Another drawing in the COHS collection, MW 2132-B, dated Dec. 7, 1939, labeled Standard Safety Rail for Light Inspection Motor Car, gives us insight to other motor cars which were contained in the railroads inventory. The notes on the drawing note the safety rails were to be installed on models Fairmont M9, M19 and the Sheffield 48B and Eclipse Model 784.

Further development of the motor car cabs and windshields took place after World War II when aluminum was again available. Manufacturers used aluminum alloy to produce windshields for the cars. In 1948, Fairmont added to its line a full aluminum cab and roof top for use on the inspection cars. These cabs could be ordered with rear windows, roll down rear curtains and side curtains. The material was more durable than the former steel cabs and was much lighter in weight.

During the years of World War II, Fairmont and other manufacturers had to modify their product lines and replace parts which had been previously been made of aluminum with steel substitutes. This was due to the material not being made available for domestic uses as it was prioritized for war production needs. The September 1942, Motor Car Performance Sheet No. 42, released by Fairmont highlights this issue. Having been forced to change the construction of water hoppers from aluminum to steel on the Fairmont OD and RO engines, Fairmont came out with a rust preventive additive to be placed into the cooling systems to counter the corrosive effects of the cooling water on the steel water hopper.

Other parts, which had been traditionally made with aluminum such as connecting rods and pistons were also substituted with steel units in May of 1943 as indicated in Motor Car Performance Sheet No. 45. Many of the Fairmont inspection cars that were built during this time period can be identified by the fact that the steel frame members have holes drilled into them to reduce the weight.

Other developments to motor cars were the application of setoff skids. These castings were bolted onto the frame of the car just behind the front wheels so that when the operator lifted the car by the rear lift handles and pulled the car over the rail, the skid contacted the rail as the car was pulled over it. This permitted the front wheels to climb over the rail more easily regardless of the height of the rail. This was particularly important when a single operator was forced to set a car off for a meet where there was not a set-off.

Another improvement occurred when manufacturers offered rail sweeps as a safety feature added to the cars. A motor car could be derailed rather easily by an object such as a piece of ballast laying on the railhead. To counter this problem a rubber blade or hose would often times be mounted to the frame of the car and located so as to extend down to the railhead surface in front of the front wheels. When the blade or hose struck a rock or other object it would kick it off the railhead, preventing a potential derailment. In 1943, Fairmont offered a new improved version which was a rubber blade that could be raised up or lowered when the blade was needed. The blade was also installed so that it wiped the rail head at an angle so as to kick the foreign object off to the side of the track.

Another added safety item was steel fenders and step plates on inspection cars. Early on many of the cars did not have fenders over the wheels, which permitted water to be thrown upward wetting tools and creating slippery footing conditions when getting on and off of the motor car. It also created a dangerous condition when unsecured tools would bounce off of the car and come in contact with the rotating wheels, which could cause a derailment or personal injury. A Fairmont photo taken in 1934 for the C&O shows the installation of a wheel guard on an M9 light inspection car which was ordered by the C&O. The C&O must have tried the metal fenders and step plates on their cars early on but ultimately decided on a different approach.

The C&O instead used a series of metal brackets and oak boards to create running boards, that covered the wheels. This in effect created deep tool trays on each side of the car and eliminated the typical metal fenders and step plate.

Stewart Bostic, Supervisor of Signals for the C&O and Chessie System had in his collection a Fairmont M19-D-5-17 motor car instruction parts list book for a unit that was delivered to Clifton Forge, Va. The book was dated

1943, and the photo of the car shows a typical M19 Series D car with a steel frame with the holes typical during the war years, and the car is equipped with metal fenders and a steel step plate.

Also, in the book, the car from the Fairmont factory was shown to be available with various ordering options, with the last version of the car identified as an M19 Series D-16. The front of the book, however, was stamped with the car being identified as a model M19-D-17. At the back of the book is stapled a mimeographed sheet, which is identified as being an M19-D-5-17 that was apparently a special order car for the C&O Railway. This option shows the traditional metal wheel guards and step plate were omitted from the construction of the car and instead replaced with wooden boards referred to as guard boards. The addendum also includes some brackets for mounting the boards and an end block for the decks of the car.

One can only theorize why the C&O preferred this arrangement of the car over the standard metal wheel wells and step plate. It may have been done for safety reasons as it created a more secure tool tray on each side of the car where it would be less likely for tools to become dislodged and be tossed out of the car. It may also have been that the railroad felt the metal fenders and step plates were a safety concern because they were slippery when wet. On the other hand the C&O may have thought the costs for these items were unreasonable or that they would not be as durable or easily replaced as the boards.

It is interesting to note that many of the cars were ordered without windshields or cabs at this time and it may have had something to do with the application of the C&O-built cabs that were applied when the unit was commissioned at Barboursville. The way the cabs were designed

C&O Motor car M-2105, a Fairmont Model M19. Rear view showing the wooden wheel guards and standard C&O steel cab sitting in storage at Clifton Forge, Va. in 1985. The C&O opted for the wooden wheel guard instead of the typical metal wheel fenders and step plate offered by Fairmont. This created a deeper tool tray on the car sides. Also note the hand lantern storage bin attached to the rear of the metal cab roof. (C. W. Ford photo)

it would have been much easier to mount them onto the flat guard board than the curved fender surface of the standard car.

The sales records for the C&O, which cover the period from 1927 until 1987, clearly show that most cars went directly to the reclamation plant at Barboursville, West Virginia, before going to their destination on the railroad. At Barboursville the cars were checked out, assigned the typical C&O motor car sequence number and the cab probably applied. It does appear from the records that some of the cars ordered after the late 1940's were ordered with cabs installed by Fairmont that were designed to C&O standards and specifications.

Throughout the 1940's the manufacturers also offered new comfortable seating to the cars, improved brake shoe materials, improvements and refinements in the carburetors and engines. In 1954 Fairmont introduced a new twin cylinder RK series engine to be made available for the M19 inspection car and S2 Series section car. By late 1959 Fairmont simplified its motorcar M19 line to offer one basic chassis and in 1960 it did the same with its section car offerings for

the M14 light duty section car and the S2 Series standard duty section car.

In its 1961 catalog Fairmont did offer two new gang cars in the A4 and A5 series. In 1967 it also offered a new version of the M-19 inspection car referred to as the MT19 and MT14 light duty section car powered by an air cooled Onan engine with a transmission rather than the traditional belt drive. This was a radical step considering both cars had been powered by the Fairmont two-cycle water-cooled, belt-driven power plant since their inception.

By the 1950's the little motorcars that had become so prominent on America's railroads had been refined to the point that there was little left that could be done to improve them. Reviewing the Motor Car Performance Sheets released by Fairmont to its customers from the 1950's on, there are few improvements in the motor car product line. The sheets from this time period on reflect more the development of other railroad product lines and less about the motor car. It was no secret that the little cars were living on borrowed time, something the manufacturers had realized as early as the late 1940s. Things were changing.

A Fairmont Model M9 motor car for the C&O showing metal wheel guards and step plate. Photo dated May 21, 1934. (Used with permission from Harsco Track Technologies)

CHAPTER FOUR

Brief History of Fairmont Railway Motors Company

The 1936 exhibit at N. R. A. A. Trade Show held in Chicago showing Fairmont Motor Cars and the Fairmont powered coach at the right of the photo. (Used with permission from Harsco Track Technologies)

The history of the Fairmont Railway Motors Company is so rich that it could occupy an entire book on the subject by itself. To understand the importance of this company and the role it played in the development of the motor car a brief history as it relates specifically to motor cars must be examined in order to understand how they developed.

As Fairmont became a major producer of motor cars within the railroad maintenance-of-way industry, producing by some estimates over 73,000 of these machines, they also became a major supplier of motor cars to the C&O Railway. The majority of cars that survived into the last years of use on the C&O into the Chessie and CSX era were predominately built by Fairmont.

Thankfully the company was a good steward of preserving their corporate history and much of the material in this chapter comes from a history of the company written by employee Orlin Foss entitled "History of Fairmont Railway

Motors Inc.". Mr. Foss retired in 1976 and the document was continued up until 1979 at which time Fairmont was acquired by Harsco. Many of the corporate documents, photographs and other records survive today at the Martin County Historical Society, located in Fairmont, Minnesota thanks to the efforts of Harsco Track Technologies.

If it had not been for a railroad employee who was a section man and lived in the area around Fairmont, Minnesota the history of the railroad motor car might have been very different. Fred Mahlman Sr. worked as a railroad section hand and like many he worked long, hard, physically demanding hours. At the end of these grueling work days he then had to physically exert himself by pumping his handcar back to Fairmont, an activity even when rested requires great strength and energy. He surmised that the gasoline engine could somehow be adapted to the hand car he used every day at work to free him of this arduous task.

Fred Mahlman, Sr., second from the left on his section car equipped with Fairmont Machine Company Motor. (Used with permission from Harsco Track Technologies)

Mr. Mahlman saw an advertisement from the Cushman Company of Lincoln, Nebraska for a 4 hp. motor that could be attached to power grain binders. He received information from Cushman but he soon learned that a local company could supply what he was looking for. The Fairmont Machine Company started by two men, Horace E. Woolery and Victor St. John in 1907, manufactured one cylinder engines locally in Fairmont. Fairmont sold many of the units for agricultural use such as pumping water and other farm chores and then for use in industrial applications such as power for saw mills. Mr. Mahlman purchased one of the 2 horsepower engines and mounted it on his motor car. At first the unit did not fulfill his expectations, so he went to the superintendent of the machine shop and asked them if they could produce a unit that would meet his needs.

The superintendent and Mr. Mahlman would take the car out on weekends and after the workday to make improvements to the concept. Mr. Mahlman was asked to document his use of the car, what its capabilities were and to produce a report of his activities. In turn this information was put into a report, which was then sent out to several railroads for their review.

When Mr. Mahlman started to receive so many requests for information that it became overwhelming he persuaded the Fairmont Machine Shop to respond. Soon orders were coming into the Fairmont Machine Company at such a high rate, that the company could not produce the little motors fast enough.

On June 1, 1909, H.E. Woolery and Victor St. John the original founders of the Fairmont Machine Shop met with Frank E. Wade, H.W. Sinclair, Clason St. John, H.P. Edwards, A.R. Rancher, George H. Snyder and William M. Hay to discuss the future of the company. The newly incorporated company was called the Fairmont Machine Company and it was started with $50,000 capital. Mr. Frank E. Wade was elected as the president of the new company.

The newly formed company produced engines ranging from 2, 2 1/2, 3, 4, 5, 6, and 10 horsepower that had a three year guarantee. The advertisements reported the engines to be the "Mighty Fairmont Engine." The new engines were built on the hit-and-miss principle with approximately one third of the moving parts of the typical gas engine; simplicity of the design was the concept. Soon the engines were distributed to forty-eight railroads which encompassed every state.

By 1910 the little Fairmont engine was being used by over one hundred railroads and the company produced its first manufactured motor car. On Jan. 11, 1915 the name of the company was changed to the Fairmont Gas Engine and Railway Motor Car Company.

In 1917, the company used a new vehicle for getting out the word about its products. "Wade's Work" was a monthly technical publication with information about the Fairmont engines. This lead to a later publication called "Right of Way" and to a series that ran for many years, referred to as Motor Car Performance Sheets, that were first released in February of 1935 and lasted through the 1960's. These publications

Photo of Frank E. Wade, the first president of the Fairmont Machine Shop, on what is believed to be the first application of a Fairmont gas engine to a handcar.
(Used with permission from Harsco Track Technologies)

were distributed to the railroad officials to keep them abreast of changes in product designs and offered maintenance instructions for customers to maintain their equipment.

In 1922 a competitive test was conducted between a Woolery Machine Company motor car and a Fairmont motor car on the Santa Fe Railroad at Topeka, Kansas. The Woolery Machine Company was started by H.E. Woolery who was one of the original founders of the Fairmont Machine Company but left Fairmont in 1917 to go out on his own.

In the test the Fairmont motor car won out. This is interesting, because a previous test had been conducted a few years prior in LaCrosse, Wisconsin without the knowledge of the Fairmont Company. Allegedly the test had been conducted against a Fairmont motor car that had been tampered with so as to skew the results. When Fairmont President Frank Wade learned of the test, he is reported to have hired a Pinkerton detective to locate the compromised Fairmont car to make repairs to the unit. When the comparison test was rerun on the Sana Fe the Fairmont motor car out- performed the Woolery Car.

On Feb. 19, 1923 the name of the company was changed to Fairmont Railway Motors Incorporated. In 1928 the company switched it fiscal year from the calendar year cycle to a fiscal period of October 1st through September 30th. In March of the same year Fairmont Railway Motors made an offer to purchase, and later took ownership of, the Mudge Motor Car Company located in Chicago, Illinois. After the acquisition Fairmont continued to sell motor cars under both the Mudge and Fairmont name for approximately three years. By 1931 Fairmont no longer advertised the Mudge line of cars.

In September of 1929 Fairmont introduced the demountable motor car wheel which was discussed in Chapter Three. This development was a major item and selling point for the railroads who maintained their motor cars. The company patented the item and shortly thereafter on Oct. 29, 1929 formed a Canadian subsidiary, Fairmont Railway Motors Ltd., located in West Toronto, Ontario for the Canadian railroad market.

During the late 1920's, as the automobile started to impact railroad ridership numbers, the company, like many of the motor car manufacturers, offered a small rail bus, which seated seven persons and was powered by a Continental engine. The bus was fitted with a four speed truck style transmission and featured reversible seats, electric lights, fans and an electrical starter. The model 2210 sold well following the Stock Market Crash of 1929 as railroads were finding ridership on branch lines declining. These vehicles were a cost effective way to continue service and eliminate the costs of running a steam train.

Over the next few years Fairmont offered four versions, model 3100, 4100, 5100 and the 6100 of the little powered coaches with the largest seating 13 riders and weighing approximately 10,000 pounds. In 1937 they also constructed a large 12 passenger coach for the Washington, Idaho and Montana Railway that provided both mail and passenger service up until 1955. It was powered by a Waukesha 110 horsepower engine and was referred to as the "Potlatcher". Clearly if a railroad had a need Fairmont would build it. They were extremely good at analyzing the market and providing it with a product the railroad wanted. These little powered coaches helped to keep passenger services on lightly used branches, thanks to their lower operating costs in comparison to those of a steam engine powered train.

In 1934 Fairmont released the differential "loose wheel" axle, which permitted the independent rotation of the wheels. Since the wheel on the outer side in a curve turns

An early Fairmont motor car.
(Used with permission from Harsco Track Technologies)

Aerial view of the Fairmont Railways Motors plant in Fairmont, Minn.
(Used with permission from Harsco Track Technologies)

more than the wheel on the inside of the curve, this produced wear on the wheel and axle components. The "loose wheel" permitted the two halves of the axle to rotate independently of each other reducing the wear on the wheels, axles and bushings. Other manufacturers copied the design and the company was forced to take actions to protect its patent.

An industry survey conducted in 1938 showed that 58.8% of all motor cars in railroad service were either a Fairmont or Mudge product, an increase of 6% over a similar survey taken in 1936. Later in the year the company released its first line bulletin containing all of its motor cars. The plans to produce the document were started in 1936 but it did not come to fruition until 1938.

A test was performed in 1939 between a Fairbanks Morse Model 709 motor car and a Fairmont S2, Series E section car. The test was conducted in an area of the Rocky Mountains where the temperatures ranged from five degrees below to fifteen degrees above zero and steep grades were encountered. The Fairmont motor car came out ahead by a clear margin according to the company documents.

The company suffered tragic losses when two of its presidents passed away in the same year. On June 10, 1939, Harold E. Wade, son of the former first President F. E. Wade,

died after serving 20 years as president and general manager and a total of twenty-six years with the company. He was only 51 years old at the time of his death. Then Mr. H.M. Starett, who succeeded Wade, passed away on Nov. 23, 1939 only five months after taking the position. He was only 53 years old at the time of his death and had worked for the company for twenty-seven years. On Nov. 28, 1939 the board of directors of the company named Walter F. Kasper President.

The effect of World War II limited the availability of certain metals, and the company was forced to re-manufacture parts in steel where it had previously used aluminum. As previously covered in Chapter Three, inspection cars manufactured at this time had holes drilled into the substitute steel frame parts so as to reduce the impact of the weight increase by the substitute material. The company attempted to engineer the replacement products in a manner that would allow them to be manufactured without radical design changes so that they could be readily substituted on the cars.

Also in 1941, the company experienced the loss of much of its workforce especially when the National Guard Unit located in Fairmont was called to active duty. This occurred while employment at the company was high due to additional government wartime contracts.

A 1948 aerial view of Fairmont Railway Motors plant in Fairmont, Minn. showing figure-eight test track at plant where motor cars were test run. (Used with permission from Harsco Track Technologies)

During 1942, the company received its first order for motor cars to be used by the Army's Railway Engineering Battalions. They built motor cars that had adjustable wheel gauges that would accommodate 30",36",39 3/4", 42", 53", 56 1/2", 60", and 66" gauge as needed. The cars were designed so that in a matter of 15-20 minutes the gauge of the wheels could be changed. These cars were known as multi-gauge cars with the letters ZU added to the normal motor car series and class designations.

Fairmont was asked to build four A5 Series C gang cars to be tested at Camp Claybourne, Louisiana, Camp Shelby, Mississippi, Clovis, New Mexico and Fort Wayne, Indiana. After the Army evaluated the pilot models Fairmont was asked to quote on 160 A5 gang cars, 160 T-14 Trailers and 50 M19 inspection cars which were all to be of the multi-gauge design. Since Waukesha could not supply enough engines for the order, the company could furnish only 96 A5-ZU-A gang cars, 96 T14-ZU-A trailers and 30 M19-ZU-E inspection cars. While Fairmont built their own motors for their in-spection and section cars they did not manufacture engines for their gang cars and relied on others such as Waukesha, Hercules, Continental and Ford. Since Fairmont's line of custom manufactured motors were of the two-cycle type, having to tool up another production line to build four-cycle

engines was not deemed feasible. As a result, for their large gang cars it relied on the already established vendors of four-cycle engines.

The first cars were shipped in 1943 to Casablanca for use by the United States Railroad Division and then went into service in Algeria and Tunisia over on the North African Railways where they were used on three different gauge railroads utilizing 36", meter and 56 1/2" track work. Other units then were sent by the Army for use in France, Belgium and Western Germany.

By 1944, one out of every nine persons residing in Fairmont was employed by the Fairmont Railway Motors Company. In January of 1944 employment at the plant was 819, but by December of 1944 the number had been reduced to 493. During the fiscal period of 1943-44 a new high was established when 4,043 cars and frames were produced, and 410 engines were manufactured. Gross sales totaled $5.9 million dollars, a new record for the company.

In 1949 the company celebrated its 40th anniversary and in July of the same year it introduced the first A30 Hy-Rail unit. The unit was installed on a Willy's Overland Jeep Truck and was shipped to the L&N Railroad. A new era had begun, one that would lead to the demise of the railroad motor car. The handwriting was on the wall and the officials

A Fairmont A30-C-1 Hy-Rail made from a Willy's Jeep. Photo dated May 3, 1957. (Used with permission from Harsco Track Technologies)

at Fairmont knew to survive they would have to concentrate on this new product and other work equipment within the industry.

Another census survey conducted in 1948 by the railroad industry indicated that 78.9% of motor car users were using Fairmont or Mudge motor cars. This was compared to the same survey taken in 1938, which showed this figure to be 58.8% an increase of 20.1% in just ten years. Clearly, Fairmont was the leader of the motor car business in the railroad sector.

The 1950's brought a downturn in the motor car industry, because of labor unrest in the railroad industry. As a result, early in the 1949-50 fiscal period there was a slump. The emphasis within the company was then re-focused on railroad products that anticipated the future reduction in railroad maintenance personnel. The equipment began to be designed with the thought that gangs would have to be able to do as much or more, with reduced personnel. The company did introduce a new gang car, the A8 Hump Car, which was used to transport car riders (brakeman) back to the top of the hump at the numerous hump yards across the nation. The company also introduced the A31 Hy-Rail Inspection Car and along with it a new Hy-Rail Division was established within the engineering division of the company.

A new Hy-Rail vehicle, the A32 unit introduced in 1952, was entirely assembled by Fairmont. Prior to this, with the A30 and A31 Hy-Rail units, the Willy's chassis had been used as the basis for the Hy-Rail car.

By 1953 the increased use of trucks by railroad maintenance employees over motor cars was beginning to be felt by the company. As a result it placed more energy into the development of the Hy-Rail product line. In 1954 however, the company released its twin cylinder two-cycle Fairmont engine, which had been in development for a number of years. The M19 inspection car and the S2 section car were the first units to receive the twin cylinder unit. The cars were designated the M19 Series AA and the S2 Series AA. The extra power provided by the new twin cylinder RK engine

was well received by the railroads who ordered them. The C&O was one of these customers that ordered the new twin cylinder engine.

In 1955 Fairmont released a new product identified as the TH1 Highway Trailer, that was designed to transport a motor car via the highway to the jobsite. The trailer would be pulled by a truck, and at the work location the motor car would be rolled off of the trailer and placed on the tracks. This clearly was another indication that the company was taking steps to preserve the motor car product line by adapting to the changing conditions within the industry.

In the same year Fairmont also introduced another version of the Hy-Rail, the A34, to replace the A31 version. The vehicle was a rail-adapted Pontiac Station Wagon. The Milwaukee road purchased the first unit and additional orders were received for more units later that year.

During 1955-56 the company released a larger trailer, the TH2 similar to the TH1, that was designed to transport large gang type cars. On Oct. 1, 1956, Mr. W. F. Kasper retired after being the president since 1939. Mr. Richard G. Wade was elected president of the company. He was a third generation president of the company, as his father was Harold E. Wade who died while president, and his great-grandfather was Frank E. Wade a founder and the first president of the company.

The hydraulic A34 Hy-Rail had to be discontinued during the 1957-58 period when the 1959 Pontiac Station Wagon was introduced. The wider track of the 1959 vehicle prevented its use a Hy-Rail vehicle. The manual Hy-Rail equipment had to be applied to a Chevrolet Station Wagon, which became the basis for the new type of A34 Hy-Rail vehicle.

The company celebrated its 50th anniversary on June 1st, 1959. The company held a week long open house in October, with 3500 visitors attending and they displayed the exhibits that were used for the 1959 Association of Track and Structures Suppliers Exhibit in Chicago. The company also streamlined the product line of the M19 inspection car, by offering one basic chassis and an option for one of three engines for the unit. This set the stage for similar changes to the section car offerings in 1960. The M14 and S2 cars were also standardized with a choice of three engines. The new designations for the cars were the M14 Series K, M14 Series J and the S2 Series J and S2 Series K. This trend would also be put in place in the near future for the gang series cars. Again, these were further signs that the motor car was slowly going away.

In 1960 in suburban Philadelphia, Fairmont installed a Hy-Rail kit on a full size GMC bus similar to a Greyhound unit. This action received much publicity in the written and electronic media at the time. This resulted in requests from other metropolitan areas for similar demonstrations. Whether this was done for some serious future mass transit

Sales Order B=95301	Car Class M-19-AA-4-5	Car No. 217501	Engine No. 100158
Erected By	Trans. Type	Trans. No.	Date 12/23/57
Sold to	Chesapeake & Ohio Railway Company		Type RK-B-4
Address	Cleveland, Ohio		Erected By 276
Shipped to	% RK Johnson,		Tested By 321
Address	Barboursville, West Virginia		Brake Pull Lbs.
Date Shipped	1-23-58 Via C&NW		Inspected By 321
RR Order No.	69591 Invoice No. 118092-S		Carburetor Fmt.
Paint Color	See below		Coil Stan-Test
Spec. Lettering			Magneto Type
Spec. Equipment			Magneto No.

Spec. Equipment

69613-E	G&L Assembly	Do not apply - Place in carton and strapped in tool tray of each car - See sales order.
C-48	Cable cleats	
F2958	Secondary wire	
LESS:	LESS:	
F-7332	Storage batteries	
M-28368	Switch to light wire	
46603	Alum. Supt. Angle	

.028 end play. rods O.K By 312. 12-26-57

Paint Federal Yellow S2H69 Except- Paint black entire inside & top of tool tray including wood foot boards. Paint black safety railings, wheels, brakes, lift pipes & control levers. 705# Handle Wt.

Final Inspection

Final Inspection By 312   137   Date 1-21-58   Date 1-21-58   By 312

F-215B   Record additional information on back side.

A Fairmont birthcard for M19-AA-4-5 twin-cylinder, two-cycle RK engine ordered by the C&O Railway in December of 1957. The C&O ordered several of these cars with the higher horsepowered engine. These were some of the last M19 small inspection cars ordered by the C&O. (Used with permission from Harsco Track Technologies)

evaluation or for some railroad maintenance-of-way application to get workers to the jobsite is lost in time. For whatever reason it was done, it did gain attention for the company and its products.

Two new gang cars, the A4 and A5 motor car, were put into production in late 1961. Also on Nov. 13, 1961 the company purchased the Northwestern Motor Car Company of Eau Claire, Wisconsin. The company manufactured the "Casey Jones" line of motor cars for many years in direct competition with Fairmont. As motor cars sales were starting to dwindle one might wonder why the company made the purchase this late in the game. However Northwestern's motor car line was not the item of interest for Fairmont. Rather Northwestern's other railroad product lines, which Fairmont did not manufacture were wanted additions to the existing Fairmont product lines. As a sign of the change taking place, motor car sales for 1961 were 33% of the total sales for the company, which were $ 4.6 million dollars. Of this amount, export sales represented 23% of the company's total volume.

Fairmont de Mexico was created in 1963 to expand the Export Division of the company. The company built a wholly owned subsidiary plant in Mexico City, Mexico. The first units shipped to the plant were a M19 Series H inspection car, one ST2 Series K section car and one TT11-E push car which were all built to standard gauge. Export sales for the

1962-63 period totaled $428 thousand dollars which was about one-third of the company's total overall export sales of 1.4 million dollars.

Two Fairmont Hy-Rail units were used in 1964 to film a television commercial for the Shell Oil Company. The commercial was shot on location on the ATS&F Railway and was shown on national television. The month of February, 1965 was record breaking for the company. The Chicago and Northwestern Railway purchased 79 International Harvester Hy-Rail units and 93 Hy-Rail kits, which resulted in sales of over 1 million dollars for the month, the largest ever booked by the company.

The company introduced the MT19 Series A inspection car and the MT14 Series L section car in 1967. This represented a significant change for the Fairmont motor car line in the inspection and section car categories, as the engines were not manufactured by Fairmont. These traditional motor cars were now powered by Onan air cooled engines and the units were provided with transmissions rather than the typical belt drive that had been on the cars since their inception. During this time period the section car line was reduced to one offering, the newly released MT14 Series L eliminating the S2 series of section cars that had been so popular during the heyday of the motor car in the typical section house.

PUSH CARS AND TRAILERS

T9 Series B
Load Capacity: 1000 lbs.
Weight: 280 lbs.

For use with light cars hauling material that is too bulky to carry on car. Also makes a good push car for small loads. Aluminum alloy frame, 14 inch wheels, and 1 - 3/16 inch axles. Deck 44⅝" x 48¾". Four wheel brakes available. Complete details in bulletin 592.

T9 SERIES B

T19 Series B
Load Capacity: 2000 lbs.
Weight: 380 lbs.

Light weight for easy handling. Gives extra space for carrying material and supplies, serves as either a trailer or a light push car. Aluminum alloy frame, 16 inch wheels, and 1 - 5/16 inch axles. Deck 66⅞" x 48¾". Can be equipped with four wheel brakes. Complete details in bulletin 592.

T19 SERIES B

HIGHWAY TRAILERS

TH1 Series A
Load Capacity: 1500 lbs.
Weight: 520 lbs.

For hauling inspection and section cars on the way. Low center of gravity, minimum width, lo ramps included. Complete details in bulletin

TH2 Series A
Load Capacity: 2750 lbs.
Weight: 1200 lbs.

The safe highway transportation of gang c Strong construction with self-storing loading ra hand winch and 7.00 x 15 tires. Complete detail bulletin 689.

TH1 SERIES A

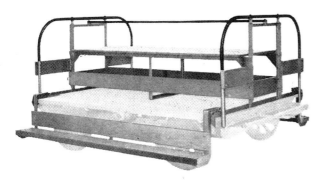

Detachable Seat and Steps Convert Push Cars to Gang Trailers

This unit may be applied to the TT1, TT11, TT5, TT6, TT7, TT12, and TT14 push cars to convert them to 20 man gang trailers. The TT designation indicates a trailer with four wheel brakes. Latches in place on push car, side steps are hinged. Weight: 300 lbs. Order reference M34236.

Fairmont Bulletin 750, dated 1957. A catalog showing the TH1 and TH2 trailers to supplement the use of trucks by railroad maintenance employees. Motor cars could be hauled to the work site. (Used with permission from Harsco Track Technologies)

T7 Series A

Load Capacity: 6000 lbs.
Weight: 520 lbs.

Aluminum alloy construction keeps weight unusually low for this class of unit. Pays off with easier handling where trailers are set on and off frequently. Deck 67¼″ x 84″, wheels 16″, axles 1 - 7/16″. Four wheel brakes available. Complete details in bulletin 617.

TH2 SERIES A

In this same time period Fairmont also released a lighter weight aluminum version of the Hy-Rail in a kit form. This reduced the weight of the equipment by almost 200 pounds.

In 1969 the company celebrated their 60 year anniversary and the sales of the company for 1968-69 were $ 8.3 million dollars. Employment at the plant was at 422, which was the highest in twenty years. Clearly despite motor car sales slowing down the company had positioned itself in the correct spot within the railroad industry. For the anniversary celebration the company again held an open house for three days, where 2,000 visitors toured the plant and were treated to lunch. The local paper, the Sentinel, published a featured supplement which was devoted to articles and photos of the Fairmont Railway Motors Company and its employees.

During 1971 the company removed from its list of products the TH series of trailers designed to haul motor cars to the jobsites, and the QBA motor car engine. It is interesting to note that in 1972 employment at the company was 422 with over 50 of those employees having 30 or more years of service to the company.

In 1973 the company began using TOFC (Trailer-On-Flat-Car) service from Blue Earth, Minnesota for export shipment of motor cars to Iran. Total bookings for the month of March of that year were 2.2 million dollars.

In March of 1975, the company completed a new foundry operation that would permit the company to be able to produce its own ductile iron castings, something it was never able to do before. With its improvements to the foundry operation, the company anticipated being able to exercise better control over the quality of castings produced and at greater cost efficiencies. In August and September of 1978, the company continued to improve its foundry operations by installing two new aluminum furnaces. Employment at the company was 675 workers, which was exceeded only during the war years during World War II.

Newly delivered Fairmont A4 motor cars at Barboursville, W. Va. shops in 1986. These eight cars in this order would be the last A4-E gang cars ordered by the railroad and the next to the last order of motor cars to be delivered to the C&O. (C.W. Ford photo)

On May 8, 1979, for the first time in the 70 year old history of the Fairmont Railway Motors Company, a strike was called by the employees of the company. The strike lasted for two months until a vote was taken on July 8, and the workers returned to the job on July 9, ending the strike.

On July 22, 1979, at 10:00 AM., the company made a public announcement that the Fairmont Railway Motors Company had merged with Harsco Corporation of Harrisburg, Pennsylvania. Fairmont was to become the 14th division of Harsco.

On April 4, 1986, Fairmont Railways Motors shipped eight Fairmont A4-E-1 gang cars, serial numbers 254647 through 254654, to Barboursville, West Virginia to the C&O Maintenance-of-Way Shops. During one of his trips to Barboursville, the author was fortunate enough to see these newly delivered cars sitting on a track outside of the shop still in brand new paint with the delivery tags hanging on the cars.

On October 6th, of the same year Fairmont shipped two A8-D-1 gang cars, serial numbers 254875 and 254876 to Barboursville, West Virginia. These would be the last motor cars ever delivered to the C&O Railway. It is interesting to note that the shipping documents still show them going to the Chesapeake and Ohio Railway Company despite the fact that the merger of the companies had taken place in February of 1973 to form the Chessie System Railroads.

In 1991 Harsco manufactured its last motor car for domestic use at the Fairmont plant in Fairmont, Minnesota. The car was an A4-E-1 gang car which was sold to the Tennessee Valley Authority. It was the end of an era for the mighty little machines that had helped to develop the railroad maintenance-of-way industry that Orlin Foss detailed in his history of the company.

The motor car was however not yet pronounced dead as Fairmont did produce two more A8-D-1 gang cars in 1998, which were exported to Chile.

Harsco consolidated their facilities in 2002, and moved the work equipment manufacturing facilities from Fairmont to their Columbia, South Carolina location. The manufacturing of Hy-Rail equipment continued at the Fairmont, Minnesota facilities until March 2011 when they were also moved to the Columbia facility. Today approximately 30 employees remain at the former Fairmont Plant located in Fairmont, MN.

In 2009 Harsco Track Technologies held a 100 year anniversary celebration at the Fairmont Plant. The company produced a book commemorating the history of the company and held a celebration at the Fairmont plant. Private motor car owners invited to the celebration brought their restored Fairmont motor cars, and the company released a CD containing images from the Fairmont company photo collection and presented copies to the attendees.

MT19 SERIES A
AND
MT14 SERIES L

AIR COOLED ENGINE

TWO SPEED TRANSMISSION

■ MT19 SERIES A   ■ ONE TO FOUR MAN INSPECTION CAR

For those who prefer an inspection car with an air cooled engine, this Fairmont MT19 is the one to specify. It is powered by a well known two cylinder, four cycle air cooled engine. The drive includes a light weight, high quality two speed transmission with a reverse. This means that the two speeds can be used to propel the car either forward or backward. Low gear gives slow speeds for detailed track inspection while high gear lets you cover the territory at a time saving pace.

The car has quality construction throughout, examples being the aluminum alloy frame for light weight strength, spring mounted axle bearings for a smooth ride, 16 inch Fairmont demountable wheels for long life, fully enclosed engine housing for safety, and aluminum extension lift handles for easier setoffs. Numerous accessories are available, see Page 3, and the car pictured above is equipped with the aluminum cab having rear window and curtain, left side seat, rail sweeps, electric lights, and manually operated windshield wiper.

FAIRMONT RAILWAY MOTORS, INC.

Fairmont Bulletin No. 903, dated 1967 for MT-19 series and MT-14 motor cars that now were powered with an air-cooled 20-horsepower Onan enigine. This was the first time in the history of the company that a non-Fairmont built engine was used on an inspection or section car. (Used with permission from Harsco Track Technologies)

FAIRMONT MOTOR CAR SYMBOLS

A good understanding of the following will be found helpful when ordering repairs and services for Fairmont Motor Cars.

Fairmont Motor Cars fall naturally into three (3) general divisions.

Inspection Cars

Section Cars

Gang Cars

Each division may include several CLASSES of cars designed for various kinds of work. For instance, in the inspection car division there are cars for one to two men and also cars for one to four men; or, in the gang car division, there are cars with 20 H.P. or 36 H.P. or 85 H.P. engines.

Car Serial No. Plate

Once selected, a car CLASS is not changed and is used through the years as a designation of similar cars. Examples:

CLASS	CLASS
M9	A5

for a certain type inspection car   for a certain type gang car.

CLASS M9 cars are one to two men light weight inspection cars; or all CLASS A5 cars are 36 H.P. — 4 cylinder — 4 speed — reversible gang cars.

EACH CLASS of car is further identified by a SERIES symbol which in combination with the CLASS symbol designates the MODEL. Example:

CLASS	SERIES
M9	A

which may be written M9 series A and is the full description of the MODEL of car. The short form of writing M9 series A is M9-A.

A given CLASS of car may be built in several different SERIES. When a new MODEL of a certain CLASS of car is put on the market, it is identified by the CLASS symbol and a new SERIES. Example:

CLASS	SERIES
M9	B

which indicates that M9 series B is a car of similar CLASS as M9 series A but is a later or different MODEL.

All Instruction and Repair Parts books are identified by the MODEL (the CLASS and SERIES) of the car. Example: Class M9 Series C — Bulletin 470.

EACH MODEL of any class of cars is further identified as to minor differences by GROUPS. The original cars of any Model are Group (1) One. Hence by combining the MODEL symbol (CLASS & SERIES) with the GROUP number we have a symbol which describes a standard motor car. Example:

CLASS	SERIES	GROUP
M9	A	1

which may be written M9 series A group 1 or M9-A-1. The latter is the short form and is preferred.

When minor improvements occur which are too insignificant to call the changed car a new model the group number is changed to identify the application of such minor improvements. Example:

CLASS	SERIES	GROUP
M9	A	2

which indicates the M9-A-2 is a car just like M9-A-1 except for some minor improvement or change.

Reference to the GROUP number will be found on the title page of each Instruction and Repair Parts book, in the Car Identification section, and in explanatory notes in the body of the parts section. Example: Bulletin No. 470 for Class M9 Series C cars, see notes page 33, references to M9 Series C Group 2 and M9 Series C Group 3 cars.

A car symbol consisting of CLASS, SERIES and GROUP always refers to the standard production car built for 56½" track gauge, which is the standard track gauge in the U. S. A.

Car Symbol Plate

FAIRMONT, in establishing the standard car, incorporates in it all necessary features for well rounded performance in the kind of service the car is intended. Many railroads, due to geographic location or climate conditions, desire certain additional equipment, which may be extra accessories as offered by FAIRMONT or may be special parts or features made up per individual railroad specifications. The application of such extra accessories, or specials, to a standard car necessitates changes to or substitution for certain standard parts. So that a car so equipped can be exactly identified for service and repair parts a SPECIAL addition is made to the standard car symbol. Example:

CLASS	SERIES	GROUP	SPECIAL
M9	A	1	1

which may be written M9-A-1-1 and indicates that some special or extra equipment has been added to the standard M9-A-1 car. Each different combination of extras or special items is given a different SPECIAL symbol and there might be a sizeable list of

Engine Serial No. Plate

specials all based on the same standard car. Example: M9-A-1-1, M9-A-1-2, M9-A-1-3, etc.

Unless a car is changed after it leaves the Fairmont factory the information on the car symbol plate accurately describes the whole car.

By consulting the repair book of a standard model car all special items will be found listed and identified by the SPECIAL symbol. Example: Bulletin No. 470 — Class M9 Series C, see pages 55 to 64.

As a check, in addition to the car symbol plate, each car carries a serial number plate. See cut. Records at Fairmont enable us to determine original date of shipment, original purchaser and other pertinent data which is helpful to our service department in filling a rush order for parts for a specific car.

Every FAIRMONT engine carries an Engine Type and Factory engine serial number plate. See cut. The engine number is very important when engine parts are being ordered, because of the practice in some railroads of transferring engines from one car to another when repairs or shop overhauls occur. ALWAYS give the factory serial engine number when ordering engine parts.

THE SYSTEM of car symbols above described has been in use exactly as described since 1938. Prior to that time the system differed mainly in the arrangement of the basic parts of the symbol and the addition of a GAUGE symbol. Example: The SERIES was put ahead of the CLASS

SERIES	CLASS	GAUGE
A	M9	A

which was written A(M9)A. There were four gauge symbols —

A for 56½" track gauge

B for 36" track gauge

C for 30" track gauge

Z for all others.

No GROUP symbols were used.

When the standard car was equipped with extra accessories or special items the SPECIAL symbol was inserted as follows:

SERIES	SPECIAL	CLASS	GAUGE
A	1	M9	A

which was written A1(M9)A. There could be any number of specials based on the same standard car.

Fairmont Motor Car Performance Sheet No. 55 dated January 1945 that discusses the Fairmont system of classification for motor car products. (Used with permission from Harsco Track Technologies)

CHAPTER FIVE

C&O Inspection Cars

C&O Fairmont M19 motor car No. M-1668 with trailer pauses on the mainline at Ronceverte, W. Va. in August 1952. (C&OHS Collection, COHS 4384)

In the early years of motor car manufacturing we know that the first complete motor car built by Fairmont was referred to as the Standard No. 1 car. This car was an inspection car meant for two people. However an examination of the sales records from the Fairmont Railway Motors Company, from 1928 until 1987 gives the researcher insight into the type of motor cars that the C&O Railway purchased from Fairmont for the period. Since the sales records for the C&O were not available for purchases from Fairmont prior to 1928 we are not able to determine which of the early produced cars the railroad may have purchased. According to the company history it was in 1910, that the first fully manufactured

car was built by the company. Further identification of the type of motor cars used by the C&O can also be gained from the Maintenance-of-Way drawings prepared by the railroad, for the windshields and cab roof tops, that were built and applied to many cars at Barboursville, West Virginia, where the main motor car shop was located.

Information taken from MW Drawing 1598-D Glass Windshield for Motor Car, in 1941, prepared by the C&O Maintenance-of-Way Engineer's Office suggests that the C&O utilized inspection cars from three manufacturers. The three companies listed are Sheffield who merged with Fairbanks-Morse around 1918, Kalamazoo Railway Supply

Side view of an early Fairmont M18 motor car. Photo dated Oct. 14, 1926. The early motor cars were crude machines. (Used with permission from Harsco Track Technologies)

and Fairmont Railway Motors. Drawing MW-1598-D refers to a Sheffield Model 41 car, which was an inspection car. The Model 41 motor car is illustrated in the 1926 edition of the Railway Engineering and Maintenance Cyclopedia. The motor car was a light inspection car capable of carrying up to three persons. It was advertised as being for use by supervisors, signalmen, and others. It was first made available in 1917 and was designed as a center loaded car that was extremely light weight.

The car was powered by a two-cylinder, two-cycle, horizontal engine and was equipped with an automatic primer to make it easier to start and get under way especially in cold temperatures. There are very few of these cars remaining in the hands of private collectors and the author has not identified any which are of C&O heritage.

Drawing MW-1598-D also indicates two Kalamazoo cars as being C&O cars, but it is possible that there is an error on the drawing. The drawing lists a Kalamazoo Model 54B car and a model 216, but Sheffield, rather than Kalamazoo, did produce a Model 54B inspection car, which is illustrated in the 1945 Edition of the Railway Engineering and Maintenance Cyclopedia.

Kalamazoo vintage 1920s Model 216 inspection car produced by the Kalamazoo Railway Supply Company in Kalamazoo, Mich. (Cliff Clements Collection)

The Sheffield Model 54B inspection car was designed for 1-4 persons for easy lifting by one person with a lift weight of only one hundred pounds. Its appearance looks very much like a Fairmont M19.

The Kalamazoo Model 216 inspection car was manufactured in both a Model 216 and a 216L. The Model 216 car was a longer car than the Model 216L and was equipped with 17" wheels and a single cylinder, two-cycle water-cooled motor. The car was equipped with a flywheel type magneto ignition system. The drive mechanism was provided by a multiple disc clutch that furnished a friction drive between the rear axle and engine. A chain drive was provided between the clutch and the rear axle.

In 1968 Mr. Cliff Clemments, a long-time C&O Historical Society member, inquired from Kalamazoo about parts for a Model 216 motor car on behalf of the Ohio Railroad Museum. In its reply the company sent him a book containing part listings and operating instructions, but indicated that the prices in the book were from the 1920's and if he needed updated prices to contact the parts department!

The other supplier of inspection cars to the C&O Railway was Fairmont Railway Motors. In the years 1928-33 it appears that most of the cars purchased from Fairmont were section cars. Records in 1928 do indicate that one Fairmont M19 Series A car and one Fairmont MM19 car were purchased. The MM19 car was equipped with a magneto ignition system, where the M19 had a battery ignition system utilizing dry cells.

The fact that few inspection cars were purchased from Fairmont during this early period could have been due to the railroad focusing on providing cars for the section gangs at that time, or perhaps they were purchasing inspection cars from another vendor. What we can see from the sales records is that from about 1933 on the railroad purchased the M9 and M19 inspection motor cars from Fairmont at fairly regular intervals and often times in large quantities.

The Fairmont M9, which was the smallest inspection car offered by Fairmont seems to have been first offered in 1926. Review of the photo logs kept by the company indicate the first photos of an M9 car were recorded in January of 1926.

Fairmont, in their 1928 sales literature, classified their motor cars into four categories, Inspection Motor Cars, Section Motor Cars, Heavy Duty Section Cars and B&B and Extra Gang Cars, but by 1933 they had reduced this listing to just three categories eliminating the reference to Heavy Duty Section Cars.

The first order placed by the C&O Railway for an M9 motor car according to the sales records available shows up in 1934, when the railroad purchased three of the M9 Series A cars.

The M9 was advertised in Bulletin 303D, which was for the "B" series of the one-man inspection car, meaning some product update had been done to the car's design over the

A Fairmont Model MM9 one or two man inspection car with starting crank suited for track inspectors or maintainers. Photo dated 1927.
(Used with permission from Harsco Track Technologies)

was primarily marketed for use by track inspectors and signal maintenance personnel, and other uses where the number of riders was limited.

The M9 version of the car was equipped with the Fairmont OD, single cylinder, two-cycle, water-cooled engine rated at 5-8 horsepower mounted with cushioning springs to minimize power impulses to the rider. The car was capable of twenty-eight miles per hour with a load of five-hundred pounds and could carry up to six-hundred and fifty pounds if speed was limited to 15 miles per hour. It is no wonder that the little machines were often referred to as "speeders" by the railroaders that used them. It came with a battery powered ignition that utilized four dry cells and a spark coil or a "buzz box" as they were often referred to. The engine was the same unit that was used in five other Fairmont cars at the time, a selling point used by sales personnel. This was a savings to the railroads, in that they would not have to stock as many parts in their inventory.

previous "A" series version, as a one man inspection car. Fairmont Railway Motors had a very distinctive identification system for their cars and a copy of Motor Car Performance Sheet No. 55, dated January 1945 is included to explain the system used.

The car utilized an endless belt drive system with an idler pulley, which meant increased safety in starting the car, fewer parts, and a simple drive train that was easily replaced when the belt would wear out. Fairmont advertised that the belts in properly maintained cars could last for 40,000 miles.

Though the car could seat two people, the company advertised it as "One-Man Lightness". The car weighed only 425 pounds with handles extending to the rear. Using the mechanical advantage with the motor weight at the other end, the lift required was only eighty-five pounds. The car

The frame of the car was made out of strong aluminum alloy manufactured by Alcoa, and eighty-nine other aluminum parts were part of the car, allowing the weight to be

Fairmont

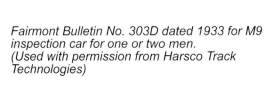

Fairmont Bulletin No. 303D dated 1933 for M9 inspection car for one or two men.
(Used with permission from Harsco Track Technologies)

Engine and Transmission

SAME ENGINE IN SIX CARS

This engine is also used in three other cars: two M14 Light Sections; the "59"; and two M19 Inspections, with the exception of hopper, condenser and controls on the steel frame M19. One stock of spare parts thus covers **six** different cars. All except minor installation fittings are identical.

Note self-centering brake shoes: accurate screw adjustment for wear. Shoes are steel-faced, far outlast soft aluminum.

Also observe convenient location, safe support of removable, two-way (only 3-lb.) starting crank.

LONGER LIFE PAYS FOR M9 CAR

Besides saving hundreds of dollars in time during its many years of better service, it is reasonable to expect this car to save enough in over-all cost (initial cost plus all repairs) to eventually replace itself.

This saving results from Fairmont cars lasting years longer, also needing fewer repairs (and these at nominal prices).

WHY M9 CAR WILL LAST LONGER

(1) Aluminum alloy frame; (2) torpedo-proof wheels; (3) simple, endless cord belt transmission; (4) water cooled, medium speed engine lightly loaded; (5) 24 years' experience building cars to last and satisfy.

WHY IT HAS AMPLE HORSEPOWER

Low H. P. means: (1) excessive time on the road; (2) steep grades, heavy winds, high altitudes or hot climates require a greater transmission reduction which speeds up and rapidly wears out the engine while still further reducing car speed, cutting mileage and available working time between runs.

WHY LESS FUEL, FEWER REPAIRS

Continuing the discussion on page 3, this engine retains every advantage of previous models, viz.: long-lived compression-tight Ringseald crankshaft packing; patented clean-firing, smooth-running throttle; three-ball-bearing crankshaft; water cooling system not damaged by freezing.

The water extends back of the ports, cooling piston and top rings throughout their entire stroke; permits a better fit and higher compression than practicable in air-cooled engines: nets more power, less wear.

CONDENSER CUTS WATERING 90%

It turns the steam back into water, uses it again and again. Some M9 cars run a week without replenishing. Test cock shows winter water level, forestalls overfilling.

ENDLESS BELT, TIMKEN CONTROL

Endless Cord Belt outlasts chain and sprockets, also costs less to replace.

One finger pulls lever, easily starts car: the control pulley has Timken bearings.

Fairmont Bulletin No. 303D showing engine and endless belt transmission (take off extra letter on transmission) to the pulley on the rear axle. (Used with permission from Harsco Track Technologies)

kept to a minimum. The car also utilized Timken bearings in both the wheel bearings and for the idler pulley. The car was outfitted with rail skids to aid in setting the car off of the track.

The early version of the car came with stub axles for the front wheels thereby eliminating a full length steel front axle and saving eleven pounds of weight. In later years this arrangement was redesigned on the cars and they were modified to include a full front axle.

The two-piece wheels made of malleable iron on the car were advertised as "Torpedo-Proof". This was important, because many of the earlier motor car wheels would not stand up to the explosion of a torpedo signaling device, often applied on the rail in the old days to signal a stop. This would result in damage to the wheel, which could cause a safety hazard potentially derailing the car or causing fragments of the wheel to be projected. In the days before the demountable wheel a damaged wheel would also probably mean a long walk back to the section house.

A number of extra equipment options were available for the car such as, hose type rail sweeps, a front windshield, a headlight, a 10 inch warning gong, a muffler, seat cushions and cover. These items could be ordered by the railroad as they saw the need. During these early years a cab for the car was not available, but would be offered in the later years.

It is also interesting to note that some M9 cars purchased by the C&O around the 1940's were ordered with a Fairmont cab that is often referred to as a "V Nose" cab due to its distinctive shape. It appeared on some M9 Series F cars delivered in 1946 and was listed as an optional Cab Top, Part # 46247E, which is a different part number than the cab illustrated in the M9-F Bulletin No. 527 issued by the company. A few of these "V Nose" cars are in the hands of private motor car collectors. Why these cars received the "V Nose" cab not the fabricated steel cab at Barboursville Shops is a mystery.

The M9 motor car over its history would undergo several updated releases. M9 motor cars were released as M9 Series A,B,C,D,E,F and the last release the M9-Series G, which was released in 1946.

Over the years the M9 motor car kept mainly the same basic design features. Many improvements were made such as the roller bearing ROC engine, the Weatherseald Timer, Fairmont C-5 carburetor, full axles with tapered roller bearings, spring mounted axle bearings, demountable steel 1/4" cold formed steel-wheels, larger fuel tank, upgraded bladed rail sweeps, aluminum cab and windshield options. Generators were added and an alternator electrical system was made available to the basic car in later years.

According to the sales records from Fairmont, covering the period from 1933 to 1956, the C&O Railway had pur-

C&O M9-F with V-nose steel cab privately owned and restored. Pre-restoration photo showing steel cab with typical C&O wooden wheelguards rather than steel fenders. (Courtesy Bill Dittmann)

chased 147 of the M9 cars. During the 1955-56 fiscal year, the C&O purchased a total of 7 of the units. The last M9-G-2-9 car was purchased on June 13, 1956 and shipped from the factory on Aug. 27, 1956. The car number on the order was listed as 213,885 and the engine number was 93,300.

The M19 was the other common inspection car purchased by the C&O railroad. The first record available in the sales data indicates that an M19 Series A car was purchased in 1928 along with an MM19 (magneto equipped) series car. No additional cars appear to have been ordered after that until 1933. From this point on the M19 inspection car was heavily purchased by the railroad.

The M19 Series A car in 1928, had a very different drive system that was built upon the design that was applied to the power kits that were added to the old hand cars. An endless cord belt was used from the single cylinder, two-cycle, 4-hp water- cooled motor to the rear axle pulley. However, instead of the idler pulley arrangement, which was adopted by Fairmont for their design, the slack in the belt was taken up by an arrangement where the engine was mounted on a sliding base. When actuated by a lever, the engine slid back on the base and took out the slack in the belt. This served as the clutch mechanism for the drive system for the car. By the release the Series B car the M19 would receive the standard 5-8 horsepower Fairmont engine.

The car was physically larger than the M9 version and was advertised as being able to carry 2-4 men. On the early versions of the car the wheels were 16", two piece pressed steel wheels, that were demountable. The wheels were held together by 12 bolts that allowed the replacement of the tire

only. This style of wheel had been used on the M19 since 1923. The early M19 motor cars were also available with a 14" wheel, which reduced the weight of the car. These wheels in the subsequent versions of the car were changed to 16" when the D series of the car was released in 1935. The 16" wheels adopted with this release were the cold pressed steel wheel introduced by Fairmont in 1929.

Frame construction consisted of both wood and steel in the early release of the car in 1928. With the Series C release of the car the frame was fabricated of steel, but in later versions of the car starting with Series D in 1935, the frame was changed to aluminum alloy. The sliding base motor drive system was also changed with this release of the car and the drive mechanism adopted the idler pulley endless belt arrangement, eliminating the sliding engine base.

The weight of a typical M19 Series F car was listed at 610 pounds which required a 98 pound lift using the rear handles. This car, while heavier than the M9, was clearly still a car which could be easily managed by one person.

The M19 series motor car underwent many of the same changes over the years and was offered in the M19 Series B,C,D,E,F, and H. Options made available included many of those offered for the M9 series, including various cab options including a steel cab in 1935, aluminum windshield in 1947, and a full aluminum cab in 1948. No records exist where the C&O ordered any of these aluminum cabs and the standard C&O steel cabs appear to have been fitted to these cars. Some of the M19 Series F cars ordered appear to have been purchased with the Fairmont steel "V" Nose" cab which was offered as an option. Other enhancements including the RO engine, alternator electrical systems, lighting packages, seats, and improved rail sweeps were all options which became available during the development of the car.

C&O M9 No. M-2001 resting in its tool house in May of 1986. The motor car was assigned to signal maintainer Neely who showed the author how it had been repowered by the Barboursville Shop with a Briggs and Stratton engine using a snow mobile transmission and clutch. (C. W. Ford photo)

C&O M9 No. M-1698 in the scrapyard at the C&O motor car shops in Barboursville, W. Va. in May 1986.
(C. W. Ford photo)

A unique version of the M19 was offered by Fairmont which included a reversible transmission arrangement on the car. It was referred to as an MR19. The car never seemed to gain widespread use by the C&O Railway though. This may have been due to the C&O preferred, for safety reasons, the cars to be traveling in a forward direction only or perhaps the more complex drive arrangement would add issues that they did not want to deal with from a maintenance standpoint.

A major change in the M19 product line came in 1954 when Fairmont offered the two-cylinder, two-cycle RK Series motor. It was made available on the M19-Series AA car and the S2, Series AA Section car. According to the sales records in 1955-56 the C&O purchased twenty-two of these cars. These were some of the last C&O M19 motor cars purchased by the railroad.

By 1959 Fairmont made a significant change in the M19 motor car line offering one basic chassis for the car with three engine options. This was an indication that the end of the road for the little cars was looming and the Hy-Rail was making inroads. In the 1957-58 fiscal years the C&O purchased two M19s and the records do not indicate any other M19 cars being purchased after that.

Fairmont was not done yet and in 1967 made a major change to the M19 car. It offered the first M19 Series T car which utilized an Onan air-cooled, four-cycle motor which had a 20 horsepower rating. This was a major departure for the company which had relied on its own two-cycle, water-cooled engines for the life of the product line. This car included a multi-speed transmission with both forward and reverse capabilities. The final drive to the axle relied on a chain instead of the typical endless belt drive.

In reviewing the Fairmont sales records, C&O purchases of the MT19 units could not be found. It is possible that one of the other railroads incorporated into the Chessie System or CSX may have purchased some of these units, but none were seen on the railroad or in the scrap piles during the 1980's when the cars were being retired.

The M19 car served the C&O Railway very well during the course of its history. It was a workhorse and the records reflect they were purchased in quantities two to one when compared to the M9 model. During the 1970's and 80's during the last years of these machines, the shops at Barboursville, experimented with re-powering the units with air-cooled Briggs and Stratton engines using a snow mobile clutch mechanism.

One such unit was located at Prince, West Virginia and operated by signal maintainer Neely, who is now a supervisor in the New River area. He stated the little car would get up and go. In private ownership the C&O M19 car is the car which has survived the most and been restored by motor car enthusiasts who own C&O cars.

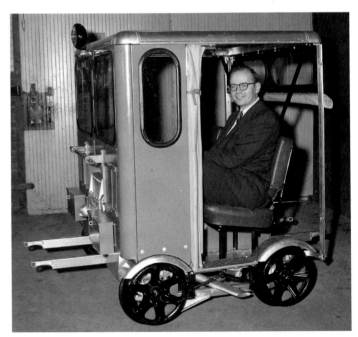

An M9-G with President R.G. Wade. The unit he is sitting in on Jan. 1, 1958 has Fairmont engine No. 100,000. The car is shown with the Fairmont aluminum cab that was offered after 1948. The C&O did not purchase these cabs for the inspection car M9 and M19, preferring their own steel cab with wooden wheel guards.
(Used with permission from Harsco Track Technologies)

C&O Fairmont M19 No. M-1823 with trailer carrying tools and supplies on Big Sandy Subdivision in the Spring of 1954. (C&O Ry. photo, C&OHS Collection, CSPR 10025.202)

Fairmont Bulletin No. 136D, dated 1925 shows sliding base engine mount on early M19 motor cars. This arrangement pre-dated the later use of an idler pulley to take the slack out of the belt. (Used with permission from Harsco Track Technologies)

An M19-F car with full aluminum cab and metal fender guards. The C&O apparently preferred its steel cab over this more common Fairmont cab. Note that the car has blade type rail sweeps to push objects off of the railroad that might derail the car. Photo dated May 23, 1949. (Used with permission from Harsco Track Technologies)

(Left) C&O M19 No. M-1178 and another motor car sitting on an overgrown track out of service and destined for the scrap pile. The cars were located in the yard at Hinton, W. Va. in 1986. (C. W. Ford photo)

(Right) C&O No. M-1241 in 1986 sitting off the track at F Tower in Fostoria, Ohio. Note the rounded roof style at the cab top versus the flat angled style on many cars. (C. W. Ford photo)

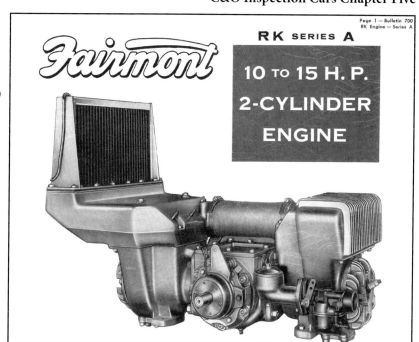

Page 1 — Bulletin 700
RK Engine — Series A

RK SERIES A
10 TO 15 H. P.
2-CYLINDER
ENGINE

Fairmont Bulletin No. 700 for the Fairmont RK Series A engine, twin cylinder two-cycle engine was released in 1954 and could be ordered in a M19 or M14 motor car. The engine offered an increase in horsepower over the single-cylinder version. (Used with permission from Harsco Track Technologies)

(Above) C&O signal maintainer Bud Huff with M19 No. M-1964 on the James River Subdivision in 1975. The young lad looking on as maintainer Huff examines the slide fence is COHS member Chris Wiley. The author would later photograph M19 No. 1964 sitting at Clifton Forge, Va. in 1984 waiting for disposal (left). (Courtesy of Aubrey Wiley)

(Left) C&O M19 No. M-1964 and M-1765 stored at Clifton Forge, Va. in 1984. Note that M-1964 has a rolled edge aluminum cab top versus the standard C&O angled steel cab roof. M-1964 that was assigned to maintainer Bud Huff has an unusual application of a grab iron at the top of the cab front at the roofline. (C. W. Ford photo)

C&O M19 No. M-1479 front view at Eagle Rock, Va. in 1988. (C. W. Ford photo)

C&O M19 No. M-1741 at the C&O reclamation shop motor car scrap yard in 1986. The author purchased four C&O cars as scrap units in the mid-1980s. The remaining cars at Barboursville were scrapped in 1987 at Mansbach Metals when the maintenance-of-way repair shop was moved to Parsons Yard in Columbus, Ohio. (C. W. Ford photo)

C&O M19 No. M-1954 in 1988 at the maintainer's tool house in Thurmond, W. Va. Maintainters Meadows and Clinebell pose with their motor car for the author during one of his photo trips.
(C. W. Ford photo)

Motor car No. M-1194 with two trailers is seen here parked beside the C&O depot at Maidens, Va., while it was being torn down on July 7, 1973. Perhaps the trailers were being used for part of the work.
(T. W. Dixon, Jr. photo, C&OHS Collection, COHS 39864)

Two men move a motor car across the tracks at the Ronceverte, W. Va. yard on Aug. 8, 1969. The car has side curtains and rear enclosure to keep out the cold winter of West Virginia. (T. W. Dixon, Jr. photo, C&OHS Collection, COHS 38965)

Motor car No. M-1963 is parked at the C&O depot at Shadwell, Va. on the Piedmont Subdivision amid the clutter from the oil company that was leasing the depot after the removal of the agent. This was a common scene along the C&O in the 1970's as the cars were being removed from service. (T. W. Dixon, Jr. photo, C&OHS Collection, COHS 39822)

CHAPTER SIX

C&O Section Cars

WS-2 Mudge (Fairmont) section car. Fairmont acquired the Mudge Motor Car Company in 1928. Photo dated Oct. 27, 1928 (Used with permission from Harsco Track Technologies)

In the early years the railroad's emphasis on motor cars centered on the section gangs and the work they performed. Since the section gang was the basic work element of the railroad Maintenance-of-Way Forces, these cars were paramount for the day-to-day track maintenance needs. Reviewing the drawings prepared by the C&O Engineering Department for the motor car cab installations again, we can see the types listed for section cars.

C&O Drawing MW D-5834-B Standard Metal Cab Top for Light Section Cars, dated July 30, 1946, identifies several section cars by various manufacturers and refers to them as light section cars. The following cars are listed; Sheffield Model 53, and the Fairmont S2 Series, D and E cars.

This is in contrast with the earlier C&O Drawing MW-1598-D , Glass Windshield for Motor Cars, dated March 22, 1941, which distinguishes between standard section cars and heavy-duty section cars. Drawing MW D-5834-B identifies the Mudge WS-2, Mudge WS-3, Fairmont S2, Sheffield 44, 44-B and even the Fairmont A6, A3 and A2 cars. We will look at the Fairmont A Series motor cars in chapter seven as they were classified by the manufacturer as gang cars but

it appears the C&O referred to them as section cars, which probably reflects how they were used. At the time the drawings were prepared, the Fairmont S2 was utilized by the C&O Railway in both the Series D and Series E versions of the car.

Section cars by the various manufacturers at the time typically could seat from 6-8 men on a car designated as a light section car. Heavy-duty section cars could seat from 10-12 men and pull up to two trailers loaded. The cars weights could range from approximately 900 to 1,400 pounds.

The Sheffield Model 40-B was built as a successor car to the Model 40 car. It was listed as a section car and was constructed of automobile type pressed steel utilizing channel and tubular members to reduce its weight but at the same time increasing the strength of the frame. The engine was two-cylinder, opposed, four-cycle, air-cooled engine and the transmission was a friction type design. By 1945 the car was described as a heavy-duty motor car by its manufacturer and the car weight was 1,235 pounds. The car had four speeds and the transmission was capable of both forward and re-verse direction.

Mudge WS-3 heavy-duty section car with belt drive and the two-speed transmission with eight horsepower, water-cooled engine. Sold until 1931 by Fairmont after they acquired the Mudge Motor Car Co.
(Used with permission from Harsco Track Technologies)

The Sheffield Model 53 was listed by the manufacturer as a light-duty section car, with an 8-13 horsepower engine with an overall weight of 930 pounds. The lift weight of the car was one-hundred and twenty pounds, which Sheffield advertised was light enough for one man to handle. Sheffield touted that the little car was big enough for a full size section gang, but small enough to serve as a track inspection or Foreman's car.

The Eclipse 784 was another offering in the Sheffield line after the merger with Fairbanks-Morse when Sheffield was offering basically the same cars under both names.

In 1928 the Fairmont sales records for the C&O indicated that early on the C&O purchased the Fairmont/Mudge cars WS-2 and WS-3. During the three year window after Fairmont acquired Mudge, Fairmont was selling both the

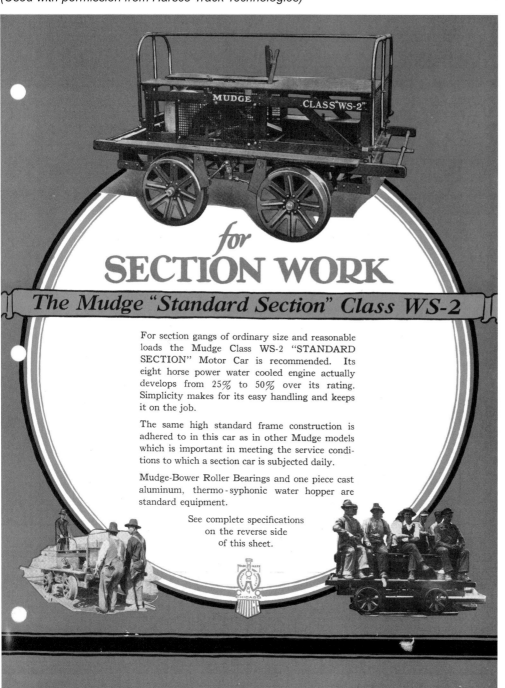

for SECTION WORK

The Mudge "Standard Section" Class WS-2

For section gangs of ordinary size and reasonable loads the Mudge Class WS-2 "STANDARD SECTION" Motor Car is recommended. Its eight horse power water cooled engine actually develops from 25% to 50% over its rating. Simplicity makes for its easy handling and keeps it on the job.

The same high standard frame construction is adhered to in this car as in other Mudge models which is important in meeting the service conditions to which a section car is subjected daily.

Mudge-Bower Roller Bearings and one piece cast aluminum, thermo-syphonic water hopper are standard equipment.

See complete specifications on the reverse side of this sheet.

An advertisement for the Mudge WS-2 standard section car from the late-1920s. The C&O drawing MW-1598-D identifies the installation of a windshield to these section cars in the C&O inventory.
(Used with permission from Harsco Track Technologies)

Mudge cars and their own products as well. The 1926 edition of the Railway Engineering and Maintenance Cyclopedia contains information from the Mudge Company of Chicago prior to their being purchased by Fairmont.

The WS-2 car was referred to by its manufacturer as a Mudge "Standard Section" car. The engine was listed as a two-cycle, two-port, water-cooled engine. The "W" class engine on the WS-2 and WS-3 cars utilized a belt drive on the cars. The "W" class engine was one of three engines offered by Mudge and had a 5" bore by 5" stroke which produced exceptional power and the engine only weighed 285 pounds. The company advertised only three moving parts: the crank shaft, connecting rod and piston.

The WS-3 series car utilized the same 8 horsepower rated engine, but also a two speed transmission utilizing a combination of belts and chain to the axle to give it more pulling power. This allowed the unit to pull trailers.

Both cars used wood frame construction consisting of Oak and Maple, which was common on the early motor cars of the era. Other features included safety rails, lifting handles, wheel guards over the wheels, and brakes on all four wheels. In the sales records, there were no purchases of the these cars after 1928, but we know that Fairmont discontinued offering them around 1931, probably after the supply of parts obtained during the purchase of Mudge ran out. By that time Fairmont was offering its own section cars.

The Fairmont offerings in the section car classification, included the M14 and S2 series of cars. In the Fairmont sales records for the C&O the author has identified in the sales records one M14 Series A car which was purchased by the C&O in 1934. This car was shipped to Montgomery, West Virginia instead of the normal delivery to Barboursville and the record contains a note under extra equipment containing the words "wheel guards". Why this lone purchase was made is a mystery. Perhaps the C&O wanted to try the light section car to determine its suitability. All of the other section car purchases are of the S2 series of cars from Fairmont Railway Motors.

The M14 car offered by Fairmont was advertised as a light section car for six men. The car must have been popular with other railroads, because it was offered in many series and was even upgraded with the Onan engine in 1967 to produce the MT14 series of the car. Since it was not widely purchased by the C&O the author has chosen not to provide details on the specifications of the car.

There is some documentation that indicates the origins of the S2 may date back as early as 1923. The earliest literature the author has on the car is Fairmont Bulletin 197 C, dated 1928. The 1930 bulletin for the S2 "Standard Series" states the car has been offered for the past six years. The car was constructed with a wood frame, was capable of hauling up to eight men, and was provided with a 6-11 horsepower Fairmont QB series, two-cycle, water-cooled, single cylinder engine. This early version of the car did utilize the sliding

base for the engine as the means to take up the slack in the belt instead of the idler pulley which was later adopted.

The 1930 Fairmont Bulletin 197 D indicates a two-speed transmission was offered for the S2 car and had the effect of doubling the pulling power of the car. These cars were often used where grades exceeded 3%, where the railroad had a lot of curvature, or when more than one trailer was needed to be pulled.

The two-speed S2 cars had the letter T added in their Fairmont car class identification system to identify them as having the two-speed transmission. The weight of the car was under 900 pounds and by 1930 the car was utilizing the 20" Fairmont, one piece cold pressed demountable steel wheel. The 1936 Fairmont Bulletin 358 indicates the engine in the car was upgraded to the QBA which had been increased in horsepower and was now rated at 8-13 horsepower. This was an improved engine over the previous 6 horsepower version of the QB which was introduced in 1914.

With the release of the S2 Series D car in 1935 the frame of the car was no longer made of wood, but was constructed of steel with holes drilled into the frame members to reduce their weight. The weight of the car was approximately 1150 pounds which was slightly more than the oak frame version. The car had been equipped with an improved QBC engine and still utilized the 20" wheels.

With the S2 Series E cars in 1939, features such as the two-speed transmission, and the Hy-Drive were emphasized. The Hy-Drive was a Fairmont feature that raised the pulley of the belt driven car higher up off the rails so that the car could travel over high weeds and deep snow, without fouling the belt. The unit could also be configured with a sprocket reduction on the final chain drive to the axle so that the pulling power of the car could be increased for mountain grades, and other severe conditions.

Fairmont QBA engine with condenser. Rated for 8-13 horsepower. Photo dated March 9, 1938.
(Used with permission from Harsco Track Technologies)

The Fairmont

M14
Series G
LIGHT SECTION CAR

DOUBLE-DUTY . . .

Because of its light weight, this six man section car can be used safely where only two men are needed, thereby serving satisfactorily, either a full sized section gang or a minimum gang.

The new Fairmont RO 5 to 8 H. P. roller bearing engine in this car supplies enough pulling power for all six man section jobs. This car will tow 3,000 lbs. net load on a trailer up ½% grade at 24 M.P.H.

The housing seat of this steel frame M14 car is hinged at one end, so that it can easily be raised for quick access to the engine.

POWERED BY
Fairmont
Hy-Load
ROLLER-BEARING ENGINE

Copyright 1939 by

Printed in U. S. A.

FAIRMONT RAILWAY MOTORS, INC. ★ Fairmont, Minn.

M14-series G Fairmont section car, dated 1939. The M14 was a light section car and the C&O purchased and shipped an M14 to Montgomery, W. Va. in 1934. Sales records for the C&O show only one M14 being purchased. The larger S2 section car was the standard section car purchased by the C&O. (Used with permission from Harsco Track Technologies)

The Fairmont S2 (Series C)

Oak Frame Section Car

ONLY 900 POUNDS

6 TO 11 HORSEPOWER

*Fairmont S2 series C section car bulletin 197D dated 1930. The S2 series section cars were purchased by the C&O for section gang use.
(Used with permission from Harsco Track Technologies)*

Fairmont S-2 section car built for C&O Railway. Photo dated Oct. 1, 1937.
(Used with permission from Harsco Track Technologies)

In the release of the S2 Series E and Series F cars the wheel size was reduced to 16" from the former 20" wheels, and the wheels were the standard Fairmont one piece cold formed demountable wheels. The 16" wheel was offered in the S2 Series D car as an option to the 20" wheel. Other improvements such as generators, windshields, rail sweeps and warning bells were starting to be offered as options on the cars.

The S2 Series F car bulletin released in 1938 shows the offering of the car with the new RQ, 8-13 horsepower, single-cylinder, water cooled two-cycle engine. This new series of engine utilized roller bearings, which Fairmont referred to as Hy-Load bearings.

The weight of the car in the Series E version was approximately 935, pounds depending on equipment installed, which required a 145 pound lift using the extension handles. Fairmont still advertised this car as being light enough for one man to lift giving testament to the strength of the average section worker.

By 1939 an S2 Series G heavy-duty section car was also available that would accommodate 10 men compared to the 8 that the smaller S2 car could handle. This car was larger in size, weighed approximately 1150 pounds, and required a 321 pound rear lift using the lift handles. The engine was the same RQ Series, 8-13 horsepower unit and utilized the stan-

dard belt drive transmission. The car had a load capacity of 1800 pounds. This unit used the larger 20" Fairmont wheels and could be purchased with the two-speed transmission and Hy-Drive option.

The Fairmont sales records for the C&O show numerous S2 cars being purchased by the railroad. The sales records indicate that the S2 Series A, D, E, and H cars were purchased. The records show that no S2 Series G cars were purchased. The sales records indicate that twelve S2 Series H units were ordered in October of 1948 and if the files are correct they were not received until July of 1949. These cars were S2-H-1-14 cars and were the last S2 cars ordered by the railroad.

By 1960, Fairmont took steps to standardize the section car line of their offerings. They offered one basic car type of each section car class, with an option of three engines just as they had done with the inspection cars. The cars now offered in the line were the M14, Series K, M14 Series J and the S2 Series J and S2 Series K.

By the 1967-68 fiscal year for the company the S2 Series car was removed from their product line and the light section car models were reduced to just the MT14 Series L. At this point the MT14 was offered powered by the Onan air-cooled 20 hp motor instead of a Fairmont built engine. This again was a sign of the approaching demise of the section motor car.

An S2-F-1 built for the C&O. Photo dated Nov. 17, 1938. (Used with permission from Harsco Track Technologies)

Sales Order	A47046	Car Class	S2-H-1-14	Car No.	189243	Engine No.	82178
Erected By		Trans. Type		Trans. No.		Date	6/4/48
Sold to	Chesapeake & Ohio Railway Co.					Type	RQ-D-1
Address	Cleveland, Ohio					Erected By	422
Shipped to	% R K Johnson, SWE&R					Tested By	420
Address	Barboursville, W. Va					Brake Pull Lbs.	20½
Date Shipped	7-7-48	Via	CMSTP&P			Inspected By	408
RR Order No.	P-91563	Invoice No.	31842-S			Carburetor	C8
Paint Color	Paint cars and cab top federal yellow SW-H-69 except paint					Coil	Yes
Spec. Lettering	black entire inside and top of tool tray including foot					Magneto Type	
Spec. Equipment	boards. Paint black safety railings, wheels, brakes, lift					Magneto No.	
	pipes and control levers.						
	51555E Cab top (Applied).						
						Final Inspection	Dr. L.
Crated Wt.		Net Wt.		Handle Wt.		Date	
Final Inspection By	W. S.			Date	6-29-48	By	P-6-5 ¾
7-215B 283		Record additional information on back side.					

Fairmont S2-H birthcard. This was the last version of the S2 section cars purchased by the C&O from Fairmont. The last S2 Series H cars were ordered in October of 1948 and were delivered in July of 1949.
(Used with permission from Harsco Track Technologies)

Front view of an S2-F section car with C&O steel cab installed at the Fairmont factory. Photo dated Jan. 6, 1947. (Used with permission from Harsco Track Technologies)

Rear view of a Fairmont S2-F built for the C&O with a steel cab at the factory. Photo dated Jan. 6, 1947. (Used with permission from Harsco Track Technologies)

A PM section car No. 978 with a windshield and cab top that is very different from the typical C&O cab in 1954. The small rectangular plate next to the C&O 978 indicates that the car is approved for night operation by the Michigan Public Service Commission that had some regulatory control over the railroads. The MPSC was created in 1919 when the Michigan Railroad Commission was abolished and replaced with the new agency. (C&O Ry. photo, C&OHS Collection, CSPR 3597)

An early M2 Fairmont section car in 1922. The early cars utilized wood frames made from hardwoods such as oak for their basic structure. Later, the wood would be replaced with aluminum and steel frames for the cars. (Used with permission from Harsco Track Technologies)

Fairmont A2 with a section gang. The A2 was classified as a heavy duty section car that could also serve as a gang car. Photo dated June 23, 1927. (Used with permission from Harsco Track Technologies)

Fairmont S2 Series H motor car top view showing the control panel, motor, and tool tray areas. The black starting crank is visible on the top side panel. The S2 series cars featured lift handles like the small inspection cars. Photo dated Jan. 6, 1947. (Used with permission from Harsco Track Technologies)

PRINTED IN U. S. A.

The *Fairmont* S2 *Series F*

STANDARD SECTION CAR 8-13 H. P.

POWERED BY *Fairmont Hy-Load* ROLLER-BEARING ENGINE

Weight, 935 lbs.
Rear Lift, 145 lbs.

MEN WHO KNOW QUALITY . . . . .

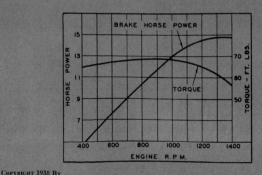

appreciate this flexible, light weight section car. The S2 series F seats eight men . . . it hauls 24000 lbs. on level track and yet it can be used as a two man car . . . because its rear lift is only 145 lbs.

Powered by the Fairmont RQ roller bearing engine, this car will give matchless, dependable service long after other cars have been scrapped.

The quality built into the S2 series F is definitely recognized by prudent track maintenance men.

COPYRIGHT 1938 BY

FAIRMONT RAILWAY MOTORS, INC. ★ Fairmont, Minn.

Fairmont Bulletin No. 394 dated 1938 is the basic motor car like the one built for the C&O (photos on page 63) without the C&O style metal cab and roof top. (Used with permission from Harsco Track Technologies)

WINDSHIELD PLAIN M29435 (above). Full width of car; protects riders at minimum cost. Easily applied in the field in a hurry. Strong material; withstands wintry gales. Rolls up for carrying.

GENERATOR OUTFIT M29433 (above). This electrical system consists of headlight (swivel mounted on front safety rail), tail lights, storage battery, and generator. The Auto-Lite generator is on hinged brackets, bolted above the engine side bearing, and is "V" belted to the pulley on the inner side of a standard "belt side" flywheel. This generator furnishes enough current for the ignition and all the lights.

DRY CELL HEADLIGHT M8404. High grade, waterproof. Cast aluminum case, 4¾" reflector, powerful bulb, and two ordinary dry cell batteries. Safe for use around gasoline. Throws 300 ft. beam or wide fan spread.

TWO SPEED TRANSMISSION. This car can be converted into an Extra Gang Car by installing a Fairmont Two-Speed Transmission. This simple device, pictured at the right, increases the drawbar pull of this car 99%. Three hardened cut steel gears run on Timken bearings. Shafts are of a fine grade of steel. Sliding gear shaft is splined. Nickel steel Wood-

AIR CLEANER M27915. Pays for itself in protecting internal parts of engine from dust and dirt. Oil bath type. Indispensable for dust-storm regions.

6 INCH HAND GONG M29430 — 10 INCH HAND GONG M29431. Durable warning signals; the larger the louder. Mounted away from tools. Operated by pull wire.

10 INCH FOOT GONG M29432. Loud warning signal operated by foot, leaving both hands free. Mounted out of the way of tools, etc.

CANVAS COVER M7951. Cars that are kept outdoors need this protection. Brown duck, treated with "Preservo" for fireproofing. Weight 10 ounces. Has eyelets for tying on car.

TOP AND WINDSHIELD M29461. Converts this car into an "all weather" inspection car. Inspection parties will appreciate the protection offered by this arrangement. Side curtains roll up when not in use. Auto windshield wipers can be mounted on the ⁷⁄₁₆" plate glass windshield windows.

HIGH TENSION MAGNETO. Choice of Robert Bosch or new Wico. Both have ball bearing driving shaft. When magneto is wanted on new car, order SM2 car series F. Be sure to specify make of magneto desired.

FAIRMONT SAFETY COUPLER M11668. Links trailer to motor car. Strong ¾" rod with self closing malleable catch. The last word in safety.

ruff keys secure the high and low gears and drive sprocket to the countershaft. Gear case is semisteel, cast in one piece, insuring correct alignment of shafts and bearings. High grade, sturdy roller chain and steel cut sprockets. Installation is simple. When ordering, specify model of car, diameter of wheels, and track gauge.

WINDSHIELD WITH WINDOWS M29434 (above). Adequate protection in bad weather. Deflects wind away from operator. Windows allow full vision. Easily applied in the field. Can be folded for carrying.

CONDENSER A1073. Very useful in hot climates and for steep grades. Constantly condensing the steam back to water, eliminates loss of water by boiling away.

RAIL SWEEPS M25465 (above). Clears rails of stones, twigs, and light snow. Air hose held in front of wheels automatically swings out of the way when car is being set off track.

HY-DRIVE M29465 (at left). Two sprockets and a chain to the drive axle raise the axle pulley high enough to safely pass over high weeds and deep snow. A decided advantage for use in parts of the country where excessive weeds interfere with the normal belt drive. Sprocket reduction provides extra pulling power for mountain grades, logging roads, and unusually severe conditions.

ACCESSORIES

Fairmont S2 Series F accessories available from Fairmont for the motor car in 1938. These optional items could be specified by the individual railroad as they saw fit. (Used with permission from Harsco Track Technologies)

A section motor car is parked in the middle of this typical C&O scene at Quinnimont, W. Va. in June 1975, beside the classic standard tool house and motor car shed. (T. W. Dixon, Jr. photo, C&OHS Collection, COHS 38997)

CHAPTER SEVEN

C&O Gang Cars

The Fairmont A2

Heavy Duty Section Car

Fairmont Bulletin No. 205D dated 1928. A Fairmont A2 car that was referred to as a heavy duty section car rather than a gang car. (Used with permission from Harsco Track Technologies)

The largest of the motorcars purchased by the C&O and other railroads were known as gang cars. Fairmont Railway Motors offered gang cars in the following versions, A3, A4, A5, A6, A7 and A8. Identification of these cars can be very difficult as the author discovered when selecting photos from his collection for this book, since none included the builders plate data. Some cars like the A8-D-1 series because of its large size and unique wheels are easier to identify.

The problem with trying to identify the other gang cars produced by Fairmont is that physically they all look alike. While there were differences, for example one might have

had a Ford engine or the other had a Hercules or Waukesha engine, without examining the actual details of the car it is hard to tell the units apart in many cases.

Fairmont also listed an A2 car in 1928, but the car is referred to as a heavy duty section car and not as a gang car. Fairmont Bulletin 205 issued in 1928 for the A2 car, also listed in the category of B&B and extra gang cars the A4 and in the large extra gang car category the A5 car.

There is no indication that the C&O Railway purchased the A2 car, however it is possible that they could have been purchased before 1929. What is interesting is that the first purchase of a gang car is identified in 1930 with the purchase of the A6 Series A car. In 1936 another A6 car was purchased along with some A3 Series A cars. Starting in 1938, the railroad began buying the A3 Series C and A3 Series D cars and purchased different variants of it up through 1945. In 1945 the C&O began buying the A5-Series Gang Car and made purchases of them up through 1970-71.

No other gang cars appear to have been purchased from Fairmont until April, 1984, when they purchased two gang cars: an A6 Series F car and an A4 Series E car. Both of the cars were shipped to Barboursville, West Virginia according to the records.

The 1926 Edition of the Railway Engineering and Maintenance Cyclopedia calls one of the cars illustrated in the Fairmont product line the "Fairmont Extra Gang Motorcar." In Fairmont records examined for this book the same photo exists and refers to the car as the A2 car, which was available in the AT2 version with the two-speed transmission. As has been previously noted this car was considered a heavy duty section car capable of carrying 12 men, so it is possible that with the two-speed transmission it was used for gang car service. Fairmont Bulletin 204C, dated 1928 is an advertisement for the ST2, MT2 and AT2 cars, and seems to support the notion these cars were really section cars with two-speed transmissions. The literature states that when these cars were equipped with the two-speed transmission it made them suitable for gang use because of their ability to pull larger trailer loads.

Fairmont Bulletin 251 dated 1928 lists that at that time A4 and A5 gang cars were available from Fairmont. There is no information for the first two A6 Series A cars ordered in 1930 and 1936. Information is available for the A3 Series B and A3 Series C car which the C&O started to purchase regularly from 1936 on.

Fairmont Bulletin 365, dated 1937, provides the data for the A3 Series B car, which was referred to by Fairmont as a B&B Extra Gang Car. The car was equipped with a Hercules, four-cylinder "L" head engine rated at 20 horsepower. The car was provided with a four-speed transmission with forward and reverse directional gear. A drive shaft transferred the power from the engine to the transmission. The car was capable of developing a speed of 27 mph.

Another feature of the car was its ability to travel at a slow speed of 2 mph, which allowed the car to be used as a fire extinguishing car for firefighting use and for stringing wire for the pole lines. The frame of the car was made of steel, which was bolted together. Fairmont touted the bolted frames on many of their cars as making it easier to replace a damaged part, and that a bolted frame allowed some flexibility of the frame members thereby relieving structural stress.

The car weight was approximately 1,480 pounds depending on how the car was equipped and had a load capacity of 2,000 pounds. The seating capacity of the car was listed as eight men. The rear lift required to take the car off of the track was 330 pounds. The car was advertised as being able to pull two trailers with 11,700 pounds of material; or three trailers, 60 men and 2,000 pounds of tools, equipment, and material. The body of the car was built of White Oak and the car used 16" X 5/16" cold formed Fairmont demountable wheels. There were many options available for the car including a windshield, top and windshield, turntable (allowed two men to set on or off), side steps which increased the seating to 10 men, and an electric starter.

With Fairmont Bulletin 403 in 1938, the Series C version of the car was released, which the C&O started purchasing in 1939. A review of the Series B and Series C car bulletins

B & B AND EXTRA GANG CAR

Weight 1480 lbs.
Rear Lift 330 lbs.

Fairmont Bulletin No. 365 dated 1937. The C&O purchased many of the A3 series gang cars. The car was powered by a 20 horsepower Hercules, four-cylinder engine with a four-speed forward and reverse transmission. (Used with permission from Harsco Track Technologies)

does not reveal any substantial revisions to the car other than the Series C car was a little heavier and the drawbar pull chart was revised.

The C&O continued to purchase the A3 Series C car up until 1945, when it purchased the newly released A3 Series D version of the car. With the release of the Series D car the engine in the car had been replaced with a four-cylinder, four-cycle, water-cooled Waukesha engine which was rated at 17.4 horsepower. This engine replaced the former 20 horsepower rated Hercules engine. Other than the engine change there were not any other substantial changes in the design of the D Series of the car.

In 1945 the C&O began moving away from the A3 car and began to purchase the A5 Series C. The A5 Series C car had been out since 1938 and was equipped with a 36 horsepower, four-cylinder, "L" head four-cycle Waukesha engine. The car was capable of more loading than the A3 up to 3,000 pounds and was advertised with a capacity of eight men. The drawbar pull for this car was substantially higher and the bulletin says that the car was capable of pulling 13 trailers loaded with 260 men at 30 mph.

The other features of the frame and body of the car were very similar to the A3 but the car was 300 pounds heavier weighing in at 1,800 pounds. The physical dimensions were very similar to the cars the C&O purchased in the 1948 period. The next gang cars were not purchased until the years 1968-71 when the A5 Series E model, released in 1966 arrived. The cars in this time period still utilized the Waukesha four-cylinder engine.

The next gang cars were not ordered until 1984 when the C&O purchased four A6 Series F-4-16 cars, which were equipped with a Ford six-cylinder, 115 horsepower engine. These cars were capable of 3,500 pounds capacity and utilized 20" X 5/16" wheels. They were capable of seating 10 men, had a spring-mounted frame and a four-speed transmission providing forward and reverse gears. The drawbar pull for these cars again increased significantly over the former A5 Series D cars that the railroad had previously purchased. The A6 Series F car had been released by Fairmont in 1956 and was produced until 1985.

In 1984, the C&O purchased one A4 Series E-1 car. These were very similar to the other gang cars purchased: designed for up to eight men, capacities of 3,000 pound loads with a Ford, four-cylinder, 43 horsepower motor and four-speed transmission. They had 16" wheels and the weight of the car was 2,000 pounds.

In 1986, another order was placed on March 19, for eight A4 Series E-1 cars which were shipped on April 4, 1986. These would be some of the last gang cars purchased for the C&O, which at this time was part of the Chessie System Railroads. The author was fortunate enough to have visited Barboursville, West Virginia at that time and was able to photograph these last cars in 1986.

The last series of gang cars purchased was in 1986, when the railroad purchased two A8 Series D-1 cars on February 9, which were not shipped until Oct. 6, 1986. The A8 Series D car was the largest gang car built by Fairmont. They were capable of a 4,000 pound load and up to 14 men. The cars were equipped with a Ford, six-cylinder engine with a 121 horsepower rating. They had a sprung frame, hydraulically operated turntable for turning the car or setting it off, disc brakes and 20" heavy duty wheels. The cars were available with a Fairmont steel cab, windshield wipers, electric horn, rail sweeps, lights and other options.

One of these cars was purchased by the Stewartstown Railroad Company in 2010 from the Brown Railroad Equipment Company located in St. Louis, Missouri. President David Williamson of the railroad first saw the car labeled with TMC 707 stored in Fairmont, West Virginia in the late 1980's. This is inconsistent with the author's photographs of other motorcars during the CSX era, (late 1980's) when he observed motorcars receiving MTC and MTCR designations. Why this car had the designation different is not known. This numbering replaced the typical C&O or Chessie System numbering system that had existed for years. The railroad purchased the car and restored it and is currently using it for track work and giving rides to the public. Where the other A8-D-1 car ended up is not known.

Shortly after the last purchases were made in 1987, the maintenance-of-way facility at Barboursville, West Virginia, was shut down and moved to Parsons Yard, located in Columbus, Ohio. The remaining inventory of motor cars located in the bone yard at Barboursville, were crushed and placed into gondolas to be delivered to Mansbach Metals located in Ashland, Kentucky, to be scrapped.

The end of a long era was closing on the little speeders that had served the railroad so well for so many years. The author does not know when the last motorcars were taken off the railroad for the final time. The last photos that he has of them in use appears around 1990.

In 1998, Fairmont did build two more A8-D-1 cars seven years after the last domestic cars were built at the Fairmont, Minnesota, plant. These cars were exported to Chile according to employees of the company.

Thankfully, many of these motorcars ended up in the hands of private owners, spared from the cutting torch and are preserved and still operating today with new life breathed into them by their owners!

C&O track gang laying rail in 1950. The gang car was the work horse of the motor cars capable of pulling many trailers of tools, supplies, and materials or trailer cars of men to and from the work site. (C&O Ry. photo, C&OHS Collection, CSPR 2624)

THE *Fairmont* A3
SERIES D

- 17 Horse Power Engine
- 4 Speeds Either Way
- 2000 Lb. Load Capacity
- Propeller Shaft Drive
- Enclosed Directional Gear

B & B and Extra
GANG CAR

The A3 series D is a versatile car of remarkably low maintenance and upkeep. It is made expressly for B&B and extra gang service, for towing mowers, extinguisher cars, or trailers loaded with men or material. Because of its light weight it is also adaptable as a heavy duty section car.

The combination of a 17 horse power engine and four-speed transmission give plenty of pull for big loads or steep grades. Actual use shows this car to be safe, serviceable, and economical.

Copyright 1945 by

FAIRMONT RAILWAY MOTORS, Inc., Fairmont, Minnesota

Fairmont Bulletin No. 530A dated 1945. The A3 Series D gang car was purchased by the C&O in 1945 and the newest version of the A3 gang car had a Waukesha 17.4 horsepower engine that replaced the previously used 20 horsepower Hercules four-cylinder engine. (Used with permission from Harsco Track Technologies)

NEW!

The *Fairmont* A6 (Series "B")

Gang Car With Ford V-8 Engine

Spring Mounted—80 H.P.

Rear lift 609 lbs. on extension handles.   Whole car 2368 lbs.

Also built with Ford Model "B" 4-cylinder 50 H.P. engine.

Fairmont Bulletin No. 333A dated 1936. An 80 horsepower gang car capable of carrying 10-11 men and capable of pulling 10 24-man trailers for a total of 250 men. (Used with permission from Harsco Track Technologies)

Fairmont A6-F-4 gang car without the optional cab at factory. Photo dated Jul. 22, 1974. The C&O ordered four of these cars with cabs in 1984 and they were still in use on the railroad in the mid-1990's. The MTC-702 shown elsewhere in this chapter is this series of gang car. Photo dated July 22, 1974. (Used with permission from Harsco Track Technologies)

Fairmont A5 Series C gang car at the factory with its steel cab built for the C&O. In the late 1940's the C&O ordered cars equipped with cabs to their specifications. The standard paint was Federal Yellow for the cab and black for the under carriage and tool trays. Photo dated Dec. 19, 1947. (Used with permission from Harsco Track Technologies)

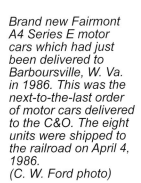

Brand new Fairmont A4 Series E motor cars which had just been delivered to Barboursville, W. Va. in 1986. This was the next-to-the-last order of motor cars delivered to the C&O. The eight units were shipped to the railroad on April 4, 1986. (C. W. Ford photo)

Fairmont A8 Series D-1 gang car. Labeled CSX TMC-707 sitting in Parsons Yard, Columbus, Ohio in 1987. This was one of two A8-D-1 motor cars that were the last motor cars purchased by the C&O/CSX at the time of purchase. Why this car had the designation TMC instead of the more standard MTC or MTCR is not known and it may have been simply a bad stenciling job.
(C. W. Ford photo)

Fairmont A8 Series D-1, formerly CSX TMC-707, in use today at the Stewartstown Railroad Co. in Stewartstown, Pa. The car was purchased from the Brown Railroad Equipment Co. in St. Louis, Missouri in 2010. (Courtesy of David Williamson)

C&O A series gang car No. M-2148 at Peach Creek Yard in Logan, W. Va. in July of 1988. A C&O tool house is located behind the speeder which is sitting off the track. (Courtesy of Herbert Parsons)

Fairmont A6-F-4 gang car at Rainelle, W. Va. on the NF&G Railroad. The car has the MTC-701 numbering scheme that was applied to motor cars during the CSX era. (C. W. Ford photo)

CSX MTC-700 with personnel trailer PCT C&O 507. The trailer cars were used to transport gangs to the work location and the motor car is painted into the CSX paint scheme. Photo was taken in 1990 at Raleigh Yard. (C. W. Ford photo)

Fairmont A6-F-4 C&O gang car labeled MTCR-702 sitting on the track at Raleigh Yard, W. Va. in 1990. The car stencil says it was placed into service in May of 1984. The car has received the new number designation that CSXT assigned to the motor cars. (C. W. Ford photo)

References

1. Barnhart, Wesley. "Velocipedes on the C&O." *Chesapeake and Ohio Historical Newsletter* Aug. 1980: 4-5. Print.

2.-13 C&O Maintenance of Way Drawing R-527, 3745-B, 5834-B, S-1691, 2132, SC-81, 1534-E, 4619-C, S-5, 2823-B, 4619-C.

14. Dixon, Thomas/Wiley, Chris. "C&O Section Tool House." *C&O Historical Magazine* Oct. 2004: 6-17. Print.

15. Fairmont Railway Motors Company Sales Records to the C&O Railway Documents. 1928-1987 Print.

16. Fairmont Railway Motors Company Bulletin 333A. A6-Series B Gang Car. 1936 Print.

17. Fairmont Railway Motors Company Bulletin 136D M19. 1928. Print.

18. Fairmont Railway Motors Company Bulletin 970 Fairmont Railway Motors Company. Bulletin. Catalog. 1977 Print.

19. Fairmont Railway Motors Company Bulletin 704A A6-Series F Heavy Duty Gang Car. 1956 Print.

20. Fairmont Railway Motors Company Bulletin 504 A4-Series B Gang Car. 1945. Print.

21. Fairmont Railway Motors Company Bulletin 204C ST2, MT2, AT2 B&B and Extra Gang Cars. 1928. Print.

22. Fairmont Railway Motors Company Bulletin 204G ST2, B&B Extra Gang Car. 1936. Print.

23. Fairmont Railway Motors Company Bulletin 403 A3-Series C B&B and Extra Gang Car. 1938. Print.

24. Fairmont Railway Motors Company Bulletin 253 A4 B&B and Extra Gang Car. 1929. Print.

25. Fairmont Railway Motors Company Bulletin 530A A3-Series D B&B and Extra Gang Car. 1948. Print.

26. Fairmont Railway Motors Company Bulletin 385 A A5-Series C Gang Car. 1938. Print.

27. Fairmont Railway Motors Company Bulletin 822 S2 & ST2 Section Cars. 1960. Print.

28. Fairmont Railway Motors Company Bulletin 303D M9-Series B. 1933. Print.

29. Fairmont Railway Motors Company Bulletin 303B M9-Series B. 1933. Print.

30. Fairmont Railway Motors Company Bulletin 556A M9-Series G. 1946. Print.

31. Fairmont Railway Motors Company Bulletin 561 The Original Demountable Wheel. 1947. Print.

32. Fairmont Railway Motors Company Bulletin 457 M19-Series D. 1941. Print.

33. Fairmont Railway Motors Company Motor car Performance Sheet No. 1. 1935. Print.

34. Fairmont Railway Motors Company Motor car Performance Sheet No. 2. 1935. Print.

35. Fairmont Railway Motors Company Motor car Performance Sheet No. 3. 1935. Print.

36. Fairmont Railway Motors Company Motor car Performance Sheet No. 4. 1935. Print.

37. Fairmont Railway Motors Company Motor car Performance Sheet No. 5. 1935. Print.

38. Fairmont Railway Motors Company Motor car Performance Sheet No. 6. 1935. Print.

39. Fairmont Railway Motors Company Motor car Performance Sheet No. 7. 1935. Print.

40. Fairmont Railway Motors Company Motor car Performance Sheet No. 8. 1935. Print.

41. Fairmont Railway Motors Company Motor car Performance Sheet No. 9. 1936. Print.

42. Fairmont Railway Motors Company Motor car Performance Sheet No. 13. 1937. Print.

43. Fairmont Railway Motors Company Motor car Performance Sheet No. 15. 1937. Print.

44. Fairmont Railway Motors Company Motor car Performance Sheet No. 19. 1937. Print.

45. Fairmont Railway Motors Company Motor car Performance Sheet No. 21. 1938. Print.

46. Fairmont Railway Motors Company Motor car Performance Sheet No. 26. 1939. Print.

47. Fairmont Railway Motors Company Motor car Performance Sheet No. 32. 1940. Print.

48. Fairmont Railway Motors Company Motor car Performance Sheet No. 38. 1941. Print.

49. Fairmont Railway Motors Company Motor car Performance Sheet No. 40. 1940. Print.

51. Fairmont Railway Motors Company Motor car Performance Sheet No. 42. 1942. Print.

52. Fairmont Railway Motors Company Motor car Performance Sheet No. 43. 1943. Print.

53. Fairmont Railway Motors Company Motor car Performance Sheet No. 44. 1943. Print.

54. Fairmont Railway Motors Company Motor car Performance Sheet No. 45. 1945. Print.

55. Fairmont Railway Motors Company Motor car Performance Sheet No. 46. 1943. Print.

56. Fairmont Railway Motors Company Motor car Performance Sheet No. 55. 1945. Print.

57. Fairmont Railway Motors Company Motor car Performance Sheet No. 59. 1946. Print.

58. Fairmont Railway Motors Company Motor car Performance Sheet No. 74. 1947. Print.

59. Fairmont Railway Motors Company Motor car Performance Sheet No. 75. 1948. Print.

60. Fairmont Railway Motors Company Motor car Performance Sheet No. 80. 1950. Print.

61. Fairmont Railway Motors Company Shipping Weight Card Records for A4-E-1, A8-D1 and M19-AA Various Dates. Print.

62. Foss, Orlin. History of Fairmont Railway Motors from 1907 to 1979. Print.

63. Knowles, C. "The Track Motor Car, Its Place in Railway Work." *Railway Engineering and Maintenance* Jan. 1930: 5-9. Print

64. Knowles, C. "What Kind of a Motor Car." *Railway Engineering and Maintenance* Jan. Feb 1930: 54-57. Print.

65. Knowles, C. "The Motor Car Power Plant." *Railway Engineering and Maintenance* April. 1930: 158-162. Print.

66. Knowles, C. "How a Motor Car is Built." *Railway Engineering and Maintenance* May. 1930: 214-220. Print.

67. Knowles, C. "Proper Lubrication, The Life of a Motor car." *Railway Engineering and Maintenance* Jun. 1930: 248-251. Print.

68. Knowles, C. "Getting a Spark." *Railway Engineering and Maintenance* Jul. 1930: 295-298. Print.

69. Knowles, C. "The Care of Motor Cars." *Railway Engineering and Maintenance* Aug. 1930: 339-342. Print.

70. Knowles, C. "How to Secure Efficient Operations for a Motor Car." *Railway Engineering and Maintenance* Sep. 1930: 376-379. Print.

71. Knowles, C. "Operating Motor Cars Safely Part I." *Railway Engineering and Maintenance* Oct. 1930: 416-419. Print

72. Knowles, C. "Operating Motor Cars Safely Part II." *Railway Engineering and Maintenance* Nov. 1930: 482-485. Print

73. Knowles, C. "Operating Motor Cars Safely Part III." *Railway Engineering and Maintenance* Dec. 1930: 546-549. Print

74. Parson, Wayne. "Fairmont Centennial Anniversary." *NARCOA Setoff* Jul./Aug. 2009: 12-14. Print.

75. Pattison, T. "Selecting Sites for Tool Houses." *Chesapeake and Ohio Lines Magazine* Nov. 1930: 16-17, 77. Print.

76. Railway Engineering and Maintenance Cyclopedia. 2nd ed. Chicago: Simmons-Boardman Publishing Co. 1926: 340-359. Print.

77. Railway Engineering and Maintenance Cyclopedia. 6th. ed. Chicago: Simmons-Boardman Publishing Co. 1945: 24-40. Print.

78. Sapp, Leon. The North American Section Car. 2011. Print.

79. Sapp, Leon. "Buda Foundry and Manufacturing." *NARCOA Setoff* Jan./Feb. 2010: 18-19. Print.

80. Sapp, Leon. "Brief History of the Motor car, Survey of North American Manufacturers." *NARCOA Setoff* Mar./Apr. 2007: 16-19. Print.

81. Sapp, Leon. " Fairmont Gas Engine and Railway Motor Car Company." *NARCOA Setoff* Jul./Aug. 2009: 10-11. Print.

82. Turner, C.W., Dixon Jr., T.W., Huddleston, E. L. (1986) Chessie's Road (2nd ed.) Alderson, WV: The Chesapeake and Ohio Historical Society. Print

83. Tvedten, Lenny. "A Man Named Fred." Gas Engine Magazine Volume 42, Number 5. August/September 2007: 21. Print

If you would like more information on the private ownership and operation of motor cars go to the website listed below.

North American Railcar Operators Association – 'NARCOA' - is a non-profit group dedicated to the preservation and the safe, legal operation of railroad equipment historically used for maintenance-of-way. The key phrase in this description is "safe, legal operation". NARCOA members operate their own privately owned railroad motor cars on railroads throughout the United States and Canada during railroad-sanctioned NARCOA excursions. Members travel through some of the most picturesque areas of the North American continent. Excursions vary from one-day, 25 mile trips between two towns to multi-day, 1000 mile trips covering several states or provinces! These excursions are organized by NARCOA Excursion Coordinators. All excursions are approved by and coordinated with participating railroads.

Railroad motor cars or 'Speeders' were used by the railroads to inspect the many miles of track for defects and to handle track maintenance. Speeders have been phased out by the railroads in favor of Hy-Rail Vehicles, which are standard road vehicles with retractable guide wheels that can operate on road or rail. Railfans bought the scrap speeders and organized NARCOA in the mid 1980's. Running a speeder costs considerably less than boating or golfing although some think it's a hot, noisy and smelly hobby! Some members also own and operate more modern Hy-Rail vehicles.

NARCOA MEMBERSHIP - NARCOA has over 1,700 members worldwide. Membership in the Association is open to anyone. No person is barred from membership due to race, religion, nationality, disability or sex. NARCOA welcomes everyone and it is easy to join. To obtain membership information, visit the "How to join NARCOA" page on the NARCOA web site (**www.narcoa.org**) where you can download a membership form. You can join on-line through the web site or by mail. The web site has links to membership info, planned motor car excursions, member advertisements, and to the bi-monthly Setoff magazine. In fact, the primary method of communication within the group is through this web site.

Officially, as a member you must pay annual dues. Maintenance of your membership is subject to the standards of conduct found in the rulebook and to the eligibility standards as outlined in the by-laws. Unofficially, as a member you should have a willingness to adhere to safety rules, some mechanical ability to restore and maintain your motor car, and some knowledge of railroad operations. And, most importantly, you should enjoy operating a motor car with friends who also enjoy this marvelous hobby.

NARCOA HISTORY - The organization of NARCOA was started in 1980 as a simple list of motor car owners, known as 'The NARCOA Roster'. In 1986, NARCOA organized the first private-owner motor car meet ever held. In 1987 we began publication of our official newsletter, THE SETOFF. In 1988, we were incorporated as a non-profit organization in the State of Delaware and started our insurance program. In 1989, we held the first handcar-only meet. In 1990, we started admitting local chapters. Today, we have grown to over 1,700 members worldwide.